I0517301

LYNTON AND
THE VAMPIRE
AT TAGAYTAY MANOR
NEAR THE VOLCANO
THAT SPEWED SORROW
RATHER THAN LAVA

BY
J. WAYNE FRYE

LYNTON AND THE VAMPIRE
AT TAGAYTAY MANOR NEAR THE VOLCANO
THAT SPEWED SORROW RATHER THAN LAVA

The Author

Wayne Frye's *Aaron Adams, Girl* series books and *Lynton* adventures are popular among mystery readers. He provides satirical political commentary to many Canadian newspapers, and his books on politics have created a great deal of controversy. He has written marketing/advertising textbooks, been a highly successful U.S. university hockey coach, professor, university president and served as a marketing consultant to hockey teams and motion picture companies. He has been cited for his work with inner-city gang children in the Los Angeles area and been active in the anti-globalization movement. He became a Canadian citizen in 2003 and lives in Ladysmith, British Columbia and Cavite, Philippines.

Other Books by J. Wayne Frye

Hockey Mania and the Mystery of Nancy Running Elk
Something Evil in the Darkness at Hopkins House
How Hockey Saved a Jew From the Holocaust:
The Rudi Ball Story
The Catastrophic Calamities of a Village Idiot
Fighting for Justice in the Land of Hypocrisy
Guide to Alternative Education (13 Editions)
Cataclysmic Dreams in Black and White
The Girl Who Stirred up the Whirlwind
The Girl Who Motivated Murder Most Foul
The Girl Who Said Goodbye for the Last Time
Fall From Apocalypse
Advertising Lab Manual
Promotions Workbook
Public Relations Workbook
Advertising Design
Armageddon Now
Worth
When Jesus Came to Jersey as the Son of Thunder
When Jesus Came to Canada to Lead an Indigenous Rebellion
Canadian Angels of Mercy – Nurses in Times of Peril
Points of Rebellion: Aboriginals Who Fought for Justice
Lynton Curls Her Hair
Lynton Buys a Cell-Phone and Hears the Voice of Doom
Lynton Walks on Water
Chablis: Avenging Angel for the Forgotten in the City of Lost Hope

LYNTON AND THE VAMPIRE
AT TAGAYTAY MANOR NEAR THE VOLCANO
THAT SPEWED SORROW RATHER THAN LAVA

TABLE OF CONTENTS

Note to university and high school teachers: This book is written in Canadian English, so discrepancies in the spelling of words should be explained to students. In the vocabulary section the Canadian spelling is used, and the definitions are based upon the meaning within the context of this book. It is suggested that a review of the vocabulary precede the reading of each chapter.

LYNTON AND THE VAMPIRE
AT TAGAYTAY MANOR NEAR THE VOLCANO
THAT SPEWED SORROW RATHER THAN LAVA

TO: Bruce, the best friend a man ever had.

Copyright 2014 by J. Wayne Frye

All rights reserved. No part of this book or covers may be reproduced or transmitted in any form or by any other means, electronic or mechanical, including photocopying, recording, or by any information storage and retrieval system, without permission from the author.

This is a work of fiction. Any similarity to persons living or dead is coincidental.

Catalogue Number: 2014-2453569

ISBN: 978-1-928183-03-7

Fireside Books – Victoria, British Columbia
Part of the Peninsula Publishing Consortium

LYNTON AND THE VAMPIRE AT TAGAYTAY MANOR NEAR THE VOLCANO THAT SPEWED SORROW RATHER THAN LAVA

PROLOGUE

DARKNESS

When the blood sucker conquers a soul
The succulent moaning,
Viciously ignites within.
Violent quivering brings the blood.
Pain and agony are vampiric pleasure.

In this streaming of rapture
From the vampire's dark kiss,
Comes ecstasy laden delirium,
A crimson embrace of evil
That longs for blood.

Listen to the children of the night and the sorrowful music they make. They are the walking dead, and within them is great evil as they seek the blood that sustains them. There are legends that tell of their pursuit of the liquid that brings them euphoric grandeur as they suckle like babies. Only their mouths do not clamp onto a nipple, they bite into the jugular to suck, suck, suck the liquid that drives their desire to survive another day in their world of sorrow. The

LYNTON AND THE VAMPIRE
AT TAGAYTAY MANOR NEAR THE VOLCANO
THAT SPEWED SORROW RATHER THAN LAVA

day is their tomb of despair. Ah, but the night, yes the night is illuminated with the splendour of the blood of unsuspecting victims that fall into their evil lair.

These creatures of the darkness quench their inexhaustible thirst on the living, for it is only the blood of the living that can satisfy their thirst. When they descend from the mountain of despair to prey upon the unsuspecting, there are few who are righteous enough to confront them and battle against the insipient evil. In the town of Old Bulihan, Philippines is she who has battled demons, ghosts and the most evil creature of all – man. That woman is going to face her greatest challenge, and in the process, she will learn a story of woe while nature comes into play as a violent volcano erupts, not with lava and ash, but with sorrow. Lynton Viñas is about to face her greatest challenge, and only the love of the man who adores her can keep her from sliding into the deep, dark abyss that waits for us all.

LYNTON AND THE VAMPIRE AT TAGAYTAY MANOR NEAR THE VOLCANO THAT SPEWED SORROW RATHER THAN LAVA

CHAPTER 1

MYTH BECOMES REALITY

In Tagaytay, Philippines there is an old mansion high upon a mountainside that reeks of discontent. It looks down upon the Taal Volcano, and so intense is the loneliness of the place the volcano seems to spew out sorrow rather than lava as it looks up upon a house that is not a home, because a home is place of love and comfort. There is a darkness that surrounds this place both day and night, a kind of darkness that makes a person's flesh crawl with dread.

Evil lurks about us constantly, and it is so sublime that we often don't realize that it is in our midst. The eye sees but does not comprehend. The mind is pecked by a cloud of deception, and it is as if we are barked at by a dog that cannot modulate sound. We are being attacked by evil, but are blinded to reality and fall within its realm, because we accept the magical manifestations of magicians of deception. The truth, like those weapons of mass destruction in Iraq, is hidden in a mountain of lies that people willingly accept as fact, because they refuse to utilize simple logic to see the depth of deception.

LYNTON AND THE VAMPIRE
AT TAGAYTAY MANOR NEAR THE VOLCANO
THAT SPEWED SORROW RATHER THAN LAVA

The house was called by local residents "The Place Where Evil Lives." Yet, no one had ever seen any indication there was anything nefarious going on there. Those who lived there did not appear often, in fact, they never appeared during daylight hours. Only at night would the master of the estate, Lekman Lopez venture forth and seemingly prowl the streets in a long black cloak, regardless of how warm it was; although, in the evening it was usually cool enough for a jacket. By his side would be his trusted servant, Quinton Sagrando. Now Lekman cut a dashing figure. Tall for at around six feet two inches, he had broad shoulders, a muscular build and almost glided when he walked down the dimly let town streets with the air of confidence reserved for the aristocratic. Never did he utter even a mild profanity to anyone, but, oh, his eyes were like two evil demons opening the gates to hell. If ever anyone possessed the vaunted and mystic manifestation called the evil eye, it was Lekman Lopez.

The symbolic and superstitious fear of the evil eye was intense among the very religious people of Tagaytay. The myth of the evil eye retains largely the same meaning no matter where the story is told. In its most basic form, the

LYNTON AND THE VAMPIRE
AT TAGAYTAY MANOR NEAR THE VOLCANO
THAT SPEWED SORROW RATHER THAN LAVA

evil eye is thought of as a look given to inflict harm, pain or bad luck on those who are its recipients. It is a look which clearly states evil intentions, and Lekman Lopez used it incessantly on those who dared gaze into his eyes. So mortified were the townspeople of that gaze, most avoided looking at him for fear they might be instantly struck dead from the power of his evil eye. The superstitious people believed the evil eye held enough power to bring about actual disaster for the unfortunate person who received the glare.

Now, in order to understand just where this fear came from, one must reflect on history and go back to the first mention of the evil eye in ancient Greece and Rome. There, it was believed that the evil eye was the largest threat to anyone who had been praised too much, or received admiration beyond what they truly deserved. The praised person would become so swollen with pride that he or she would bring about his or her own doom via the evil eye, which was believed to be able to cause physical and mental illness. In fact, any disease which did not have an immediate, obvious cause was thought to be caused by the evil eye. It was thought that the gods and goddesses were punishing those who had become too proud of their achievements, and destroyed them with the power of the evil eye and returned them to the ranks of the normal.

A belief in the evil eye is still widespread today, so the people of Tagaytay were not unique in their superstition. In the Holy Quran, , the prophet Muhammad warned about the dangers of the evil eye and said that taking a bath could counteract the effects of the evil eye.

Many religions hold that excessive praise will bring about the ill effects of the evil eye. Thus, instead of praising an adorable child, one is supposed to say "God has willed" the child's good lucks, or risk bringing about catastrophe for the infant. Certain Jewish sects believe that excessive praise invites retribution through the evil eye.

The Hindus believe that the eye is the most powerful point for intense energy and a fear of an evil look from the eye can make the superstitious cower in fear.

Giving the evil eye is generally ascribed to men, though women can also have the power. It is the evil eye which has been used as a reason women in ancient cultures painted their eyelids black to protect themselves from the evil eye, and to prevent themselves from eyeing another with the look.

In Europe, the myth of the evil eye originated with the idea that envious or malicious looks had the innate power to bring about bad luck, misfortune and disaster. The largest source of the evil eye was believed to be witches. Yet, those with eye colors which were rare were also seen as powerful possessors of the evil eye look. For instance, Germans feared those with red eyes. In Ireland, those with squinty eyes were feared to be evil eye sorcerers. In Italy, the double brow was another sign that one could cast an evil eye.

Like all things religious in America, the evil eye was used for patriotic propaganda as a warning that the devil was sending his henchmen to cast about among the heathens who dared turn their back on God. This evil eye would affect so many people that the nation would fall, so to ward it off, one had to not only abide by God's laws, but bow in patriotic servitude to a nation that was blessed by God.

LYNTON AND THE VAMPIRE
AT TAGAYTAY MANOR NEAR THE VOLCANO
THAT SPEWED SORROW RATHER THAN LAVA

In modern life, pop culture, and even jewellery and design; the evil eye is used in the marketplace. Who is not familiar with the phrase "the evil eye," or thought to have caught someone casting it their way at least once or twice in a lifetime? We all have experienced that sense of evil from someone at sometime. In Turkey, the evil eye is ingrained in every day life and has deep symbolism throughout the culture. The evil eye pendant is affixed to anything that is perceived to attract greed, envy or ill-will. In Turkey, you will find the evil eye symbol on currency, in homes and offices, hanging from the necks of newborn children and farm animals, and in the foundations of buildings and on money. In the USA, the evil eye does not appear often, but in a society where greed is promoted as an enviable trait, perhaps it should be more prevalent.

The myth of the evil eye makes sense in a world where 1% garners all the fame, fortune, success and praise. It is perhaps an equalizer for those of us relegated to the margins to serve the interests of the privileged and powerful. Whatever the case, those most often in the spotlight, such as celebrities, or those with success or reasons to be proud, should probably carry with them the

LYNTON AND THE VAMPIRE
AT TAGAYTAY MANOR NEAR THE VOLCANO
THAT SPEWED SORROW RATHER THAN LAVA

protection of an evil eye amulet or evil eye talisman just to be safe, according to those who believe in the evil eye. For the entrepreneur who knows about vampires it might serve him well to sell crosses to ward off vampires as well as the evil eye amulets and talisman. Had the people of Tagaytay known the truth, they would have been better served had an entrepreneur included a stake to drive through the heart of a creature from the grave, a creature that refused to die, a creature that was crusted with evil.

Of course, our story takes place in the Philippines, and it is there that the science of Usog or Balis is practiced. This is psycho-medicine in Filipino psychology (but considered just a superstition in the western world) where an affliction or psychological disorder is attributed to a greeting by a stranger, or an evil eye hex. It generally affects an unsuspecting child, usually an infant or toddler, who has been greeted by a visitor or a stranger. In some limited areas, it is said that the condition is also caused by the stranger having an evil eye, or in Tagalog a *masamang mata*, lurking around. This belief was likely passed on by the Spaniards who colonized the Philippines and were influenced by *mal de ojo* superstition. This disorder is well-

LYNTON AND THE VAMPIRE
AT TAGAYTAY MANOR NEAR THE VOLCANO
THAT SPEWED SORROW RATHER THAN LAVA

documented in the Philippines, and once affected, the child begins to develop a fever and sometimes convulsions. Supposedly, the child can be cured by placing its clothing in hot water and boiling it. In most other places, to counter the effects of the "usog" a stranger or newcomer is asked to put some of his or her salvia on the baby's abdomen, shoulder or forehead before leaving the house. The newcomer then leaves while saying: "*Pwera usog... pwera usog...*" The saliva is placed on the finger first, before the finger is rubbed on the baby's abdomen or forehead. The stranger is never to lick the child. The practice is that the stranger or visitor is asked to touch his or her finger with saliva to the child's body, arm or foot (*"lawayan"*) to prevent the child from getting overpowered (*"upang hindi mausog"*).

So, with this background, we can now began our story in earnest about how Tagaytay fell under an ancient evil that most had thought was nothing but myth. However, for the people of Tagaytay and Lynton Viñas, myth was about to become reality.

LYNTON AND THE VAMPIRE AT TAGAYTAY MANOR NEAR THE VOLCANO THAT SPEWED SORROW RATHER THAN LAVA

CHAPTER 2

THE HUMAN EQUATION

Now leave this place where evil dwells,

Where hope dies in smouldering embers.

Walk briskly with veiled steps

Through the shadowy leaves of fall.

The eerie glow of the moon

Shines through bush and oak,

As misery proclaims her path,

While the birch trees bowing low

Shed incense of discontent on the track.

How lonely the coolness of night,

As souls fill with dread

In this true place of quiet!

The evil can almost be grasped.

Yet, within Lynton's heart

A thousand nights like this

Cannot alter hope.

In Old Bulihan in the province of Cavite near Metro Manila lives a young woman named Lynton Viñas. She, along with her two friends, Channa and Ingrid, are well-

LYNTON AND THE VAMPIRE
AT TAGAYTAY MANOR NEAR THE VOLCANO
THAT SPEWED SORROW RATHER THAN LAVA

known for fighting against charlatans and exposing injustice. They have also had books written about their exploits in battling against supernatural forces, and recently had been praised for exposing a religious charlatan in a town near Tagaytay. Now Lynton, under the tutelage of her boyfriend, who was once a well-known concert promoter in the USA, had recently been enjoying success as a mall entertainer. She and her friends had taken a hiatus from the touring circuit, and after a vacation in Taal Heritage Village, where they had exposed a religious charlatan, they had gone their separate ways:

Lynton was a woman of modest means, and she lived among the hustle and bustle of the GMA section of Bulihan where the people were in constant motion day and night. She had gained fame, because Canadian author, Wayne Frye had told of her exploits in several books. Her neighbours were aware of who she was and were impressed with her reputation as a woman who fought for justice and fairness in a country where poverty was accepted as a normal condition. While the few accumulated riches, the many languished in desperation trying to make ends meet. Lynton's compassion and determination to fight for economic justice kept her in good stead among the downtrodden who cried for a crumb of bread from the table of plenty set for the powerful and wealthy. To the people who knew her, she was a champion among women – a purveyor of kindness and hope.

Money was of little concern for Lynton as long as she had the means to survive from one day to the next. She saw life as a grand and great mosaic of possibilities, but realized that far too many people were forced to always be at the bottom looking up. She longed for a system of fairness where each individual was respected and given equal opportunities with those who were born into affluence. This was a woman of great compassion and dedication to justice for one and all.

Although in a poor area, she lived in a nice condominium that was on the borderline between those of modest, but sufficient means, and those who had to struggle for sustenance. In this atmosphere, she was a venerated and revered figure who, when she walked down the street, was always greeted cheerfully by many people who either knew her personally or knew of her by reputation.

LYNTON AND THE VAMPIRE
AT TAGAYTAY MANOR NEAR THE VOLCANO
THAT SPEWED SORROW RATHER THAN LAVA

Although she lived at the end of a cul de sac on a street littered with tricycles (motorcycles with side cars), karaoke bars, and squatters in makeshift shacks, it was picturesque and solitary in its attraction for her as a woman who enjoyed being among what she called "the real people." At home in the Presidential Palace performing for politicians or in poor barangays dancing and singing for those with no power and often with no hope, she commanded respect and admiration for her talent and compassion. Thus, as she sat on her balcony one day in July, anxiously awaiting the return of her boyfriend Wayne from Canada in three weeks, she reared back in her rocker and surveyed the area as the sun was setting. There was majesty to the area filled with people who, although they struggled for survival, were imbued with an intense vitality that permeated the barangay with a homogeneous spontaneity among the citizens that made them gregarious and excited as they greeted each day with devotion and dedication to each others welfare. The road in front of her two stories, four unit condo was very old and narrow and the part in front of her home was cobblestone. Across the street was a one story four unit complex with clothes hanging up on the patios, blowing in the slight breeze that was stirring in the humid air. Beside that was a large lot with a dilapidated shack on it. Four of the 12 children that the couple had were playing among the six roosters that meandered through the dirt front yard. To her immediate right was a large three story home where a rich family that owned several neighbourhood businesses resided, electing to live among the people who were their customers, rather than live in a gated community walled off from the common people. Further down the lane, where the street ended, was a creek that meandered in deep shadow through the neighbourhood. Over the creek was a steep gothic style bridge that led into a depressed area of shanties where people lived alongside the creek. There was the real face of poverty that trapped people in a downward cycle for themselves and the children they invariably brought into the world due to religious conviction that had been pounded into them by a church that insisted that the true lovers of God would be fruitful and multiply without any regard for the disservice they were doing to those children by bringing them into a world where they, like their parents, would be, due to circumstances beyond their control, relegated to a life of poverty. The simple practice of birth control was a solution to hunger that was too often ignored.

LYNTON AND THE VAMPIRE
AT TAGAYTAY MANOR NEAR THE VOLCANO
THAT SPEWED SORROW RATHER THAN LAVA

Lynton was a woman who never wavered in the belief that all human beings were due respect in a world where most people were judged by the content of their bank account rather than by the content of their character. So when Anna, who had walked over from the shacks around the creek, yelled from below the balcony asking to come up, Lynton joyfully said, "Sure Anna, come on up and enjoy the lovely sunset with me."

Asking if she could get her something to drink, Lynton noticed Anna appeared very perplexed as she said, "No thank you Lynton. I have a very serious problem with my daughter who lives in Tagaytay, and I know you are familiar with that area, because of your recent adventure in Taal Heritage Village that was written about in the papers. You are looked upon as a real heroine around here, and I thought you might be able to help my daughter."

Lynton could not help but chuckle heartedly at being called a heroine by Anna, as she said, "I am afraid my reputation is exceedingly exaggerated. Believe me, I am no hero. I am just a woman who tries very hard to stand against any injustice in a world where the wealthy, the politicians and the corporations try to make us all their slaves. What is your daughter's problem? Her name is Lupe right?"

"Yes. Lupe lives near Tagaytay Manor, the home of Lekman Lopez. Do you know of the tales associated with that place?"

Lynton, although having been exposed often to the supernatural, was still a sceptic who never accepted anything at face value. With that in mind, she said, "I am familiar with what the rumours are, yes. However, I am afraid that tales of vampires sucking blood to nourish their quest for eternal life is a bit far-fetched for me. I know the name Lekman Lopez and that he has lived there for many years, and there have been strange deaths nearby attributed to mysterious bites on the necks of the victims. I have been exposed to many things that defy explanation, but until I see proof he has bitten someone and sucked blood from the bite, I must be sceptical of the rumours."

"I understand that Lynton, but there has been a recent biting, and that someone was seen being bitten by Lupe."

LYNTON AND THE VAMPIRE
AT TAGAYTAY MANOR NEAR THE VOLCANO
THAT SPEWED SORROW RATHER THAN LAVA

"Give me the details," said Lynton as she leaned over a bit and placed her right hand on Anna's arm to show concern.

"It all started about three weeks ago. You are familiar with Tagaytay Manor where Lekman Lopez has lived periodically for many years now. You see, Lupe lives on the opposite side of the road in a ravine that meanders down the mountainside to the shore where you catch the boats to Taal Island. She works at JolliBee Restaurant in downtown Tagaytay. Most days she takes a tricycle to work, but something happened three weeks ago that prevented her from doing so. Well, she usually works days, but because a friend who works the 10:00 PM to 8:00 AM shift wanted to change with her when her boyfriend was in town, she cheerfully agreed. However, she was unable to get a tricycle (a motorcycle with a sidecar for caring passengers) to work since it was night-time, so she wound up walking the first night. Most people always walk on the opposite side of the road, as that dreadful place where Lopez lives is rumoured to harbour all kinds of evil within its sinister walls of discontent. However, it was raining that night, and the roadway was partially washed away across

LYNTON AND THE VAMPIRE
AT TAGAYTAY MANOR NEAR THE VOLCANO
THAT SPEWED SORROW RATHER THAN LAVA

the street, so Lupe crossed over to the other side, without really thinking, and walked in front of Tagaytay Manor. It was a mistake, because what she saw has haunted her ever since."

Lynton eased back in her chair, and with intense interest, listened to each word that rolled off Anna's lips as if they were sharp thorns of malcontent being cast into the humid air in the diminishing light of the day, almost as if the words portended an ill wind about to blow into Lynton's life. Anna continued, "So, she felt, for some reason, compelled to look over to the manor and there was a window on the third floor that was open. In front of that window stood a young woman who fell into the arms of Lekman Lopez, almost as if hypnotized. He bent over her and placed his mouth on her neck, and she gave no resistance. Lupe stood transfixed at what she as observing. Just as she was about to run, Lopez lifted his mouth from his feast, turned his head toward Lupe and wickedly smiled as blood dripped from the sides of his mouth. Oh, and he gave her such a frightful look with blood-red eyes that seemed to pierce the night air and hone in directly on her, not just on her physical being, but on her soul. She was so

LYNTON AND THE VAMPIRE
AT TAGAYTAY MANOR NEAR THE VOLCANO
THAT SPEWED SORROW RATHER THAN LAVA

frightened that she could not move. She stood transfixed just looking into his hypnotic eyes that seemed to be beckoning her to walk up the drive to the manor. Suddenly, a Jeepney came roaring by and awakened her from the trance. She turned, shouted for it to stop, jumped on board and sat with the other passengers trembling from fear. They tried to console her, tried to convince her that she was probably just imagining things as no one had ever dared even look upon the manor without fear and trepidation so evil was it. She would have none of it, and got off when the Jeepney arrived in town and went directly to the police. They merely laughed at her and said she had been watching too many vampire movies and that despite all the fear in town, there was never any indication anything sinister was going on there. Lekman Lopez was just a misunderstood eccentric, according to the police."

Lynton had experienced the supernatural several times, and those times had been chronicled by her biographer and boyfriend, Wayne Frye. Yet, she maintained a healthy scepticism in regards to things that often seemed to defy explanation. She still believed in what she could genuinely see with her own eyes, and the idea of blood-sucking vampires was simply too far-fetched for her to put credence in the tale she had just heard. Still, she had an incredibly inquiring mind that was always seeking out stimulation, and this was certainly a tale that piqued her intellectual curiosity. She cheerfully told Anna that she would pay a visit to Taal, a place she dearly loved, and conduct a cursory investigation, but that she could offer no hope for a specific solution to what Lupe had seen. In fact, she indicated to Anna that what she may have seen was nothing more than just a man and woman engaging in foreplay of a somewhat unusual nature before making love.

Anna said, "It may be as you say, but my daughter knows the woman. It is a teacher, Diana Rodriquez, at the elementary school there, and she saw her a few days later downtown and noticed she had what appeared to be bite marks on her neck."

Anna, then with tears in her eyes, continued. "You see, Diana Rodriquez is where the real problem lies. My daughter noticed that she has begun to visit that house regularly, and that Diana also, for no apparent reason, keeps showing up in front of my daughter's house, where she just stands for a few minutes, staring at the home, staring at it as if she were contemplating something evil. I am afraid for Lupe, and Lupe seeems to be changing."

Lynton nodded her head affirmatively as she said, "I'll go there and check things out. No promises, just a guarantee that I will do the best I can to uncover the mystery of that house and why Diana Rodriquez is staring with what appears ill-intent at your daughter's home. I am not a miracle worker. I am just flesh and blood, but I am a tenacious seeker of justice and truth. If there is something nefarious going on, I will uncover it."

The forest around the area where Lekman Lopez lives opens in an irregular and very picturesque glade before its gate, and at the right a steep Gothic bridge carries the driveway over a stream that winds in deep shadow through the woods. Lynton observed it as a very lonely place. Looking from the bottom of the hill up at the house, the forest in which the home stands extends 1000 metres in three directions. The nearest neighbours are the squatters down the hillside that overlooks Taal Volcano. It was there that Anna's daughter lived in mortal fear of what she had observed. These poor people who eked out an existence could not afford to live in town, as they were forced to dwell on the fringes of polite society, where, when the volcano exploded, they would be obliterated almost instantly. These were the expendables of society – those who served the moneyed class that lived in splendorous luxury off the backs of those who were nothing more than modern day serfs in the new feudal system that replaced the lords of the manor with the captains of industry. Different names, but the same old disparity of income that kept most people in slavery to the privileged class.

Two kilometres west of Tagaytay Manor was the city of Tagaytay, a city that held a special place in Lynton's heart, because it was there that she spent the second two weeks of her boyfriend Wayne's first visit, getting to know the man who would capture her heart and lavish her with so much love that she was often overwhelmed with amazement.

Nearby was a ruined village with stone shacks, and an abandoned quaint little church, now roofless, in the middle of which are the mouldering tombs of some of the former residents. Though poor, somehow they managed to borrow

LYNTON AND THE VAMPIRE
AT TAGAYTAY MANOR NEAR THE VOLCANO
THAT SPEWED SORROW RATHER THAN LAVA

the money for lavish funerals and to build elaborate stone tombs to house bodies that were simply going to decay no matter where they were placed. The poor spend lavishly on death, but can never muster the funds to be lavish while alive. Lynton often watched the poor, and ached for them while at the same time seeing that they often only made their situation worse. It was not the rich who were addicted to cigarettes, but primarily the poor. The cigarette companies hocked their cancer sticks among the poor, addicting them to a drug that brought them a bit of euphoria amidst the daily grind that kept them in slavery. Lynton had shown many family members on paper the yearly cost of their addiction, but they could not muster the courage to quit. Even when she explained that they were enriching corporations which kept them enslaved, they simply shrugged their shoulders and said, "What can we do? We are just poor people and no one cares about us." Yet, Lynton cared. She cared that these people simply lined up for their own shackles and chains but did not realize it.

Looking up at Tagaytay Manor brought a cold chill to Lynton. She had already done her research on the manor. The home had sat empty for over 50 years, deserted by the

LYNTON AND THE VAMPIRE
AT TAGAYTAY MANOR NEAR THE VOLCANO
THAT SPEWED SORROW RATHER THAN LAVA

Kabian family that had come from Romania originally. Respecting the cause of the desertion of this striking and melancholy place, there is a legend which I shall relate at a more germane time. Let it suffice to say that it was deserted out of deep, appalling melancholia caused by a singularly catastrophic manifestation that brought great sorrow and misery to the Kabian family. That sorrow was evident for 50 years as it sat deserted by all mankind, no one seemingly wanting to risk living in a place that exuded within every stone a lonely cry of desperate bleakness, gloom and woefulness.

Then Lekman Lopez arrived in town one night with his servant. Since Lopez had moved in, none of the melancholia of the place had been altered. An air of doom, anguish and bitterness still cast a pall over the manor as if it was part and parcel of what was endemic to the evil that dwelled there. Ironically, across the street was an evil of a different kind – the evil of poverty as evidence by people living in squalor on the hillside. It was there where Anna's daughter Lupe lived with her husband and six children. Yes, thought Lynton, six children brought into poverty, and they would continue that cycle of poverty with their own offspring as people believed they should be fruitful and multiply without consideration for a world where poverty was as common as a bead of sweat on a person's brow in the tropical noonday sun.

As she walked toward Lupe's home, she glanced back over her left shoulder at the manor and saw standing at the third floor window an incredibly imposing figure of a man – tall, robust looking, extremely muscular but not overly so and she could not help, even though nearly 1000 metres away, notice eyes in darkness that seemed to glow like two beacons. They were enthralling, mesmerizing, almost hypnotic. Although she dearly loved her Wayne, she could not help but take a deep breath and almost shutter at what was maybe the most handsome man she had ever seen.

She began to think: "Am I trapped and unable to escape?" Was she being snared in this man's web, and were the strands vibrating with allure to keep her from breaking free. Those eyes bore in on her as she stood there in the middle of the road looking back in the darkness at those eyes that mesmerized her. Was there no escape? She felt his eyes devouring here completely, almost as if they were saying to

LYNTON AND THE VAMPIRE
AT TAGAYTAY MANOR NEAR THE VOLCANO
THAT SPEWED SORROW RATHER THAN LAVA

her "accept your fate. You will endure whatever pain I offer and enjoy it. So accept your fate, surrender yourself to me, your new obsession, your new passion, your true owner. So stroll to me and imagine how sweet your life could become being ground down beneath the heel of my towering bulk of sinewy masculinity."

Suddenly, there was a continuously loud beeping sound as two headlights bore down on her. "Beep, beep, beep" the sound reverberated in the humid night air. It was a Jeepney and she was standing there in the middle of the road. She quickly jumped to her left and nearly tumbled down the hillside, because one thing all Filipinos understood, Jeepney drivers yielded to no one – human or machine. They were the fearless warriors of the road who took no quarter and gave no quarter. As Lynton struggled to keep from falling down the hillside, the driver went careening on down the road, oblivious to whatever human toll he might have wrought. Oh, and Lekman Lopez was still standing in the window, still gazing downward, but the spell had been broken. Lynton would not look directly at his eyes now. She only glanced at them from the side, to be sure that gaze did not enthral and entrap her.

LYNTON AND THE VAMPIRE
AT TAGAYTAY MANOR NEAR THE VOLCANO
THAT SPEWED SORROW RATHER THAN LAVA

Shaking her head as if loosening the cob webs of rapturous malevolent intent, Lynton took a deep breath and realized that there was something malicious about Tagaytay Manor and Lekman Lopez. This would be an adventure that required her two trusted companions, Channa and Ingrid. A quick call to Ingrid as she strolled toward Lupe's house led to an assurance from Ingrid that she and Channa would be in Tagaytay the next morning unless Lynton required them immediately. "No," she replied. "Immediacy is not necessary, but be forewarned Ingrid, because I know how you adore attractive men. Our last sojourn here put you in the arms of a deceiver. Believe me; this man, Lekman Lopez, is far more dangerous than Bradley was."

Laughing, Ingrid said, "Do not worry. I learned my lesson. Never again will I put so much trust in a man until he proves himself to me with more than flowery words and lavish gifts. I am looking for a man like your Wayne – frugal to a fault, a bit on the homely side, out-of-shape but devoted and true to the one he loves."

Lynton replied, "Well, I'll tell Wayne about the devoted and true part, but leave the rest out."

LYNTON AND THE VAMPIRE
AT TAGAYTAY MANOR NEAR THE VOLCANO
THAT SPEWED SORROW RATHER THAN LAVA

They laughed together; Lynton disconnected and proceeded to the dilapidated shack that Lupe called home. This, thought Lynton, was the result of unfettered capitalism where all the good things only flowed to those at the top. Government did not care about these people, because their votes, if they did vote, always went to the lesser of two evils. The poor had no power and no hope, because government's job was to protect those at the top, not cater to those with no power or wealth. It was the way of a world where compassion for the downtrodden had been replaced with blame. If you were poor in the modern world, it was your own fault according to modern thinking. Get an education. Of course, the government wouldn't give you money to do that and there was no answer to the question of genes which prevented some from attaining high levels of education. Get a good job. Of course, the good jobs were reserved for the educated who came from the fast disappearing middle and upper classes, and even those were only token placements within the corporate structure that made each worker a slave to the bottom line. So, hope had been trampled under the heel of the exploiters who controlled government and made it the vassal for their greed.

LYNTON AND THE VAMPIRE
AT TAGAYTAY MANOR NEAR THE VOLCANO
THAT SPEWED SORROW RATHER THAN LAVA

Lynton knocked on a shabby thin plywood door that was held up with leather straps nailed into a 2 by 4 that was beginning to rot. One of Lupe's children, probably about 12 thought Lynton, opened the door and graciously said, "Hello" through teeth that were beginning to rot. Yeah, welcome to poverty where dental care is unaffordable, but you could be assured that the politicians' children had beautiful teeth as a result of benefits furnished by the taxpayers who could not afford the dental insurance for themselves, but were expected to provide it for the politicians and their families. Yeah, this was called democracy!

Lupe's husband sat on an old worn out sofa puffing away on a cigarette, blowing smoke in his children's faces who were sitting beside him. Lynton wondered if he ever gave any thought to how much money he could save by putting down the drug that was dispensed by a corporation that had no heart or soul, but only existed to addict people so that the executives could reap a fortune based on murdering individuals who were made into drug addicts. They were not selling cigarettes; they were selling a drug dispensing system.

LYNTON AND THE VAMPIRE
AT TAGAYTAY MANOR NEAR THE VOLCANO
THAT SPEWED SORROW RATHER THAN LAVA

Lupe was an attractive woman, but like most people trapped by poverty, she had little means to display that beauty. The dress she had on was a uniform required by her employer. Of course, she was expected to buy it as a condition of employment, so the employer made money by paying her a low wage, and then compounded that injustice by also forcing her to pay an extravagant amount for the uniform which was priced at 3 or 4 times what the employer had to pay for it. And, of course, through it all the poor clung desperately to the notion that they were luckier than the 30% of the nation that was unemployed. It was that kind of thinking that kept the poor in poverty. They were simply too scared to unionize and demand a fair wage for a fair day's work. They were unable to comprehend that in numbers there is power. If only the poor would band together and demand justice there would not be enough police, enough weapons, enough government officials to deny them justice.

Ah thought Lynton, where is Che Guevarra when you need him? Where? Dead, of course, killed at the behest of the capitalists in America, who tolerated no descent anywhere from that mantra of "free market" capitalism which, in effect, meant corporate control of the entire world and the people who produced the goods and services that made the elite rich. The workers did not enjoy the fruits of their labour. It was those who sat in their gated estates walled off from reality who reaped the benefits of others hard work.

Looking around at the stark circumstances under which Lupe and her family had to live, Lynton could not help but wonder why anyone would bring so many children into such poverty. Could they not understand the simple elements of birth control? This was an injustice to the children that was simply compounding the injustice of a society where the poor were pawns to serve the few in a system that was based on continued inequity. The inequity was the lifeblood of vulture capitalism that devoured all within its path. Poverty was fuel for an economic system based on greed that kept people fearful of losing the job that made it possible for them to survive in a system that had no reverence for the human equation.

LYNTON AND THE VAMPIRE
AT TAGAYTAY MANOR NEAR THE VOLCANO
THAT SPEWED SORROW RATHER THAN LAVA

CHAPTER 3

SOMETHING EVIL ABOUT THAT PLACE

Where Monsters Grow

Beware of the monsters
Who dwell in the mind,
Who grow in the shelter
Of shadows they find.

Beware of the demons
Who hide from the light,
Who only survive
When hidden from sight.

These creatures can thrive
Where diligence is low;
They fill in the spaces
Of what we don't know.

Beware of the monsters
That are filled with hate,
They strike out in anger
When we can't relate.

LYNTON AND THE VAMPIRE
AT TAGAYTAY MANOR NEAR THE VOLCANO
THAT SPEWED SORROW RATHER THAN LAVA

Our own ignorance darkens
The mind and the heart,
And lets the monsters
Inside to tear us apart.

The mansion reeks of despair,
Shadowy and dark on a hill.
It stands in starkness and loneliness,
As the night is solemn and still.

The witching hour is at hand
At lonely Tagaytay Manor on high.
Lekman Lopez arises from his coffin
To flap his wings and fly.

Lupe's home reeked of smoke as her husband obviously felt no responsibility for exposing the children to second hand smoke. He never bothered to look up as Lupe said, "Hi Lynton, good to see you. I apologize for being in a hurry, but I am late for work and my employer isn't very tolerant about tardiness, so could we talk on my way to work please. The Jeepney will be here shortly." She turned toward her husband and said, "This is my husband Richie."

LYNTON AND THE VAMPIRE
AT TAGAYTAY MANOR NEAR THE VOLCANO
THAT SPEWED SORROW RATHER THAN LAVA

Richie waved his hand but never took his eyes off the television, where some inane program imported from the USA was blaring loudly. Lynton cordially said "nice to meet you," but he did not respond.

What follows is a summary of the conversation Lynton and Lupe had. Some minor details have been left out, but the crux of the discussion is very specific and made Lynton aware of the fact that Lekman Lopez of Tagaytay Manor was no ordinary man. Maybe he was not a vampire, as that was a bit far-fetched, but after listening to Lupe; she was convinced that there was something sinister going on at Tagaytay Manor.

Lupe appeared traumatized by what she saw in the window that evening, and she was so frightened that she went directly to the police who laughed at her, and suggested she had been watching too many horror movies. Yet, she was so convinced of Lekman Lopez's evil intentions that she was living in fear. Like the police, her husband laughed at her and suggested that she had just seen two people playing love-making games, and that she should forget about vampires and concentrate on taking care of her family. He was tired from watching television all day and told her to do the washing and clean the kitchen, as he was going to bed. This gave Lynton the general idea that Richie was selfish, lazy and generally lacking in respect for his wife. Yet, this was not the reason Lynton was there. Anna wanted her to investigate what was up with Lekman Lopez, not teach her daughter how to handle a jerk of a husband.

When it came to Diana's explanation of the marks on her neck, she simply intonated that apparently the marks were mosquito bites. Lynton interjected that it was certainly feasible, but Lupe insisted that they were too large and too prominent to be mosquito bites. And there was something else. Diana was going to Lekman's house on a regular basis, and each time she did so, she would, after leaving, stand on the road and stare at Lupe's house for at least ten minutes. It was very unnerving, because along with that unusual occurrence, each evening when she walked down the road to catch the Jeepney for work she would see Lekman staring out the window at her. She was careful to avoid gazing into his eyes, but she could feel the stare. Lynton mentioned that she understood, because she had also encountered the mesmerizing stare.

LYNTON AND THE VAMPIRE
AT TAGAYTAY MANOR NEAR THE VOLCANO
THAT SPEWED SORROW RATHER THAN LAVA

After talking with Lynton, Lupe felt more at ease knowing that she had a woman on her side who was famous for standing against injustice, arrogance, and above all, for battling demons. Lupe, although still perplexed and scared, felt much more confident, but when she got to her job at the 24 hour fast-food restaurant that night, she was shocked when she saw Diana Rodriquez standing by the door. Diana moved toward Lupe with a determined stride that seemed to portend trouble. Diana let a sinister grin slowly creep across her lips as she approached Lupe and in an almost whisper, said, "Bringing in that demon hunting bitch won't do you any good Lupe. Nobody can help you now. It is too late for you. Have a good evening at work."

Lupe's heart skipped a beat. She froze in her tracks and the security guard was staring at her. In the Philippines every corporate establishment had an armed guard as the businesses were ever vigilant against any attempt at robbery or terrorist activity. In a society where poverty was so prevalent, where those at the top flaunted their wealth while the poor scraped by, there was always worry about just how long society could keep those on the outside looking in from demanding fairness.

LYNTON AND THE VAMPIRE
AT TAGAYTAY MANOR NEAR THE VOLCANO
THAT SPEWED SORROW RATHER THAN LAVA

Observing the consternation on Lupe's face, the guard said, "Are you OK, Lupe? Is there anything I can do for you?"

Visibly shaken, she could not utter a word. She only shook her head no, and walked into work fearful that her children would soon be motherless. She began to think that even a mighty demon fighter like Lynton was no match for Lekman Lopez, and obviously he had an ally in Diana Rodriquez. Evil had come to Tagaytay and Lupe was caught up in its web. She suffered great anxiety at work that night, but it was only the beginning of what would be a time of great tribulation and eventual realization that she was meant for something special in the world.

Lynton's usual procedure was to talk to her dear Wayne every night on Skype when he was back in Each night she always felt invigorated, because he never stopped using flowery language to show his love. This night was no different. In a soft voice he said, "Lynton I miss you so much. I am so lucky when I am with you. Getting to wake up with you by my side and gaze into those deep, dark, penetrating eyes that sparkle with a hint of mischievous intent brings me such joy. I am afforded the privilege of being greeted each day by that gorgeous smile that spreads across those succulent lips and shines a beacon of hope upon me that lights up my life and makes the blood in my veins palpitate with anticipatory delight that I am afforded the privilege of another day in your warm arms."

Lynton replied and sighed longingly, "Wayne, you better come back soon. You have me swooning with desire now."

Hearing Lynton relate the story of Lekman Lopez and what she was about to undertake filled Wayne with consternation, but he knew asking her to drop the whole affair would be an exercise in futility. She was a woman with no fear, and her devotion to the cause of justice and fair play was legendary in a country where it was often in short supply from a government that catered to the moneyed interests rather than the real needs of the people who were trapped in a cycle of exploitation by a cruel economic system.

With her iron will and determination in mind, all Wayne could say was "be careful, sweetheart."

LYNTON AND THE VAMPIRE
AT TAGAYTAY MANOR NEAR THE VOLCANO
THAT SPEWED SORROW RATHER THAN LAVA

Wayne had just bought her a new purse before leaving, and as they talked he reflected on that purse and how it represented who this extraordinary woman was. The bag was like the person who carried it, lovely. The colour pink in it represented the purity of heart she has and the compassion she shows. The small black part represented those who would defile her kindness and take advantage of her generous nature. As the prominent colour, pink overwhelmed the black, so her goodness stands out in stark contrast to the blackness that surrounds it. He fell in love with her, because she was a good and decent woman who sees wrong and cries for justice, sees suffering and tries to heal it with kindness and sees misery in the fields of despair where the majority toil in anonymity to put bread on their tables and encourages a rebellion of spirit against oppression. Yes, Lynton Viñas was an exceptional woman who had captured Wayne Frye's heart.

They both laughed and said good night. Love makes you miss someone desperately when they are away, but it also makes you appreciate more fully the time you have with them. Wayne and Lynton lay in their beds lonely for each others embrace that night, but they also were filled with the

LYNTON AND THE VAMPIRE
AT TAGAYTAY MANOR NEAR THE VOLCANO
THAT SPEWED SORROW RATHER THAN LAVA

joy of love, and they knew that their separation only solidified their longing for one another.

As was often the case, Wayne could not rest until he wrote a poem of love to his beloved and put it on Facebook, so she would see it the next day when she awakened.

> *The days with you are a delight,*
> *As love blooms and takes flight.*
> *If push came to shove.*
> *I could be martyred for my love.*
> *Love for you is my religion.*
> *My creed is love and you are its recipient.*
> *Your touch makes stars shine,*
> *And your smile is divine.*

> *So wrap yourself in my warm arms.*
> *Bright star, would I were steadfast as thou are.*
> *In lone splendour you brighten my night.*
> *Pillowed upon my fair love's ripening breast,*
> *I feel forever its soft fall and swell.*
> *Awake my heart forever in a sweet unrest.*

LYNTON AND THE VAMPIRE
AT TAGAYTAY MANOR NEAR THE VOLCANO
THAT SPEWED SORROW RATHER THAN LAVA

Still to hear her tender-taken breath,
I will swoon and love her until my death.

Vampires are all around us and we do not know it. I am
not talking about the creatures of the night that go in search
of blood, but of the corporations that suck us dry of life.
They enslave workers to the grinding machinery of
dependence for the job that puts food on the table, and the
consumer is made a slave through titillation that encourages
him or her to buy products and services that are not needed.
People are convinced by these monoliths of evil that
happiness can be bought. The corporatizing of the world
has left little choice in the marketplace as a few giant
corporations divide up market share and practice price-
fixing of monumental proportions. So, the real vampires are
the corporations that suck, suck suck until we are all
drained of hope in a world where the brass ring is always
just out of reach.

Lynton lay in her motel room, listening to the whir of the
air conditioner, thinking about poor Lupe and how she was
reduced to slaving away to support children she should
have never had, and to support a lazy man who smoked like

a chimney in the Yukon in winter. Thus was the way of the world for the poor, who were the fodder that fed the machinery of capitalism and funnelled riches to those at the top of the economic ladder.

Into this cruel economic system that had no heart and no compassion for those who lived on the fringes, walked Lynton Viñas, a woman who was imbued with a heart of gold, and who valiantly sought justice where there was none. She realized that what most people saw as chaos was simply order yet un-deciphered. She realized that we live in a dark age, when freedoms are diminishing, when there is no space for criticism, when totalitarianism—the totalitarianism of multinational corporations, of the marketplace—no longer even needs an ideology, and religious intolerance is on the rise. Lynton knew that whatever was going on at Tagaytay Manor was more than just imaginary evil. No, she did not believe in vampires, but she believed that the world was filled with blood suckers – those who sucked the life out of people for their own selfish ends. The worst blood suckers of all were the real vampires of the world – corporations without hearts or souls.

LYNTON AND THE VAMPIRE
AT TAGAYTAY MANOR NEAR THE VOLCANO
THAT SPEWED SORROW RATHER THAN LAVA

Who was Lekman Lopez? Was he a compulsive entity that wanted to do evil? Was he one of the few who felt they were beyond the reach of the law? Lynton had already battled one of those who thought they were above the law in nearby Taal Village only a few months before, exposing a religious charlatan. Now, it was a so-called vampire that had to be exposed. Before she had to battle the superstitions of some religious people in Taal Village, and now there were more superciliousness forming around the stories of a vampire.

There was never a shortage of things for people to fear. Fear is what kept people in line, made them toe the line, not rock the boat, accept their fate as inevitable. Religion always made the poor prepare for the second coming, because that is when the last would be first and the first would be last. This was used as a carrot to dangle before the poor, a promise that their misery in this life would be replaced by glorious euphoria in the next life.

People like Lupe clung to hope that the rapture would sweep them up in a cloud of happiness and shower them with riches in an afterlife. They had to be eternally vigilant against the antichrist that was going to tempt them. They must be dutiful, work hard, and never question the order of things.

Christians have been waiting on tenterhooks for the Second Coming since the Bible itself was written. Many have prophesied the exact time of date of His return and all have been wrong. Back in the mid 2nd century, Montanus convinced his followers that the 2nd coming would be during their lifetimes. Despite Christ's no show and the continuation of civilization, somehow the cult lasted for centuries. A couple of hundred years later, a North African Christian tribe known as the Donatists tried the same scam, saying everything would collapse in 380CE. Around the same time, St. Martin of Tours declared that the anti-Christ had already been born and was on His way to gaining power over the world. A mathematical Christian group called the Lotharingians were quite certain The End would be in 970CE because in that year, the Annunciation and Good Friday were on the same day. Pope Innocent III prophesied the 2nd Coming for 666 years after the rise of Islam., the year 1284. Archdeacon Militz of Kromeriz and an ascetic monk named Jean de

LYNTON AND THE VAMPIRE
AT TAGAYTAY MANOR NEAR THE VOLCANO
THAT SPEWED SORROW RATHER THAN LAVA

Roquetaillade both said it would be around 1365CE. Melchior Hoffman, an Anabaptist prophet, predicted that the world would burn in 1533CE. The Fifth Monarchy Men, a guano insane English terrorist group, said the apocalyptic battle between Christ and Satan would happen in 1666CE. George Rapp said it would be September 15th, 1829. William Miller predicted October 22, 1844. Jesus' failure to arrive is known as "The Great Disappointment". Many of his disillusioned followers went on the found the 7th Day Adventist Church, who are still patiently awaiting His return. Charles Russell, 1st President of the Watchtower Society told his fellow Jehovah's Witnesses that Jesus would be back in 1874. Rudolf Steiner maintained that from 1930 onwards, Jesus would grant certain people psychic powers to enable them to witness his presence in the "etheric plane". Herbert Armstrong, Pastor General of the Worldwide Church of God said Jesus would return in 1975. Bill Maupin managed to convince his followers to sell all of their worldly goods in preparation for Jesus' return on June 28th, 1981. Benjamin Crème stated that on June 21st, 1982 Christ would make a worldwide television announcement. Mark Blitz, Pastor of El Shaddai Ministries said it would be September 30th,

LYNTON AND THE VAMPIRE
AT TAGAYTAY MANOR NEAR THE VOLCANO
THAT SPEWED SORROW RATHER THAN LAVA

2008. Jerry Falwell said it would happen between 1999 and 2009. Harold Camping told everyone that the Rapture would happen May 21, 2011. After failing in his first predicted date of 1994, he failed again!

Conversely, many believe He has already come in the form of Sun Myung Moon, Emanuel Swedenborg, Baha u llah, Mirza Ghulam Ahmad, David Koresh, Hailie Selassie, John Thom, Arnold Potter, William Davies, George Roux, Ernest Norman, Krishna Venta, Ahn Sahng-Hong, Jim Jones, Mashall Applewhite, Hulon Mitchell, Wayne Bent, Ariffin Mohammed, Mitsuo Matayoshi, Jose Luis de Jesus Miranda, Inri Cristo, Thomas Provenzano, David Icke, Shoko Asahara, Hogan Fukinaga, Marina Tsvigun or Sergei Troop. So, yeah, thought Lynton "the last hour" – give or take a few million years was at hand. However, none of this mattered right now as people were filled with fear, especially Lupe, filled with fear of that which was not understandable. Well, Lynton was no ordinary woman. She was a human dynamo afraid of no one. Vampires? Hey she didn't believe in them, but if they were real she would find a way to combat them, and with her devoted and loyal friends Ingrid and Channa, she would destroy the evil.

LYNTON AND THE VAMPIRE
AT TAGAYTAY MANOR NEAR THE VOLCANO
THAT SPEWED SORROW RATHER THAN LAVA

Being a celebrity, when word of Lynton's presence got around to those who considered themselves the elite of the town, a grand party was planned. Lynton had no use for the elite of the world, as she preferred to mingle with the common people. She saw the elite as self-absorbed arrogant aristocrats who thought their money made them better than others. Yet, when she received an invitation to a soirée the following night at the Perrdonez Estate, she thought it best to go, if for no other reason, to decipher the feelings of the elite toward Lekman Lopez. It was a good place to start trying to explore just how others might feel about any sinister goings-on at Tagaytay Manor. She asked if it was alright to bring her friends Ingrid and Channa. Ms. Perrdonez gladly consented and thus the three woman were preparing for the party, as having arrived in the early afternoon, Ingrid and Channa , who loved to dress up, were excited about the prospects of wearing something Wayne had brought them on his last trip to the Philippines.

Now, it must be made categorically clear here that these were three extraordinarily beautiful women, and what made them all three unique was that their inner beauty even exceeded their outer beauty. Describing the three with

LYNTON AND THE VAMPIRE
AT TAGAYTAY MANOR NEAR THE VOLCANO
THAT SPEWED SORROW RATHER THAN LAVA

words is like imagining the grandeur of the Grand Canyon without pictures. It is nearly impossible to do.

Ingrid was, like Channa, tall for a Filipino, maybe 5:7. She had long, silky smooth hair that she usually pulled back in a pony tail which hung all the way down to her waist. When she walked, it would sway from side to side, flopping about sexily, as if it was a long magic wand of enticement. Her forehead was smooth with no wrinkles, and her bronze skin colour seemed to glisten in any light that reflected upon it. It actually sparkled. Yes, it sparkled as if giving off a glistening array of delightfulness that made the sun dance with glee. And her deep, dark eyes seemed to beckon men to embrace her. They appeared to be almost pleading for the ecstasy of a slow, erotic touch from a virile man who would swoon with pleasure in her arms. Her nose was not flat like most Asian noses, but a bit thin and slightly turned up. Her lips were soft, inviting, ruby red and slightly thin, and they seemed to be begging for a passionate, wet kiss. Her breasts were not gigantic, but ample enough to gently bounce up and down with a smooth, fluid motion that made men gasp as she provocatively moved toward them. Her hips flared out in a subdued way that seemed to naturally progress to long, vibrant silky smooth legs that were perfectly proportioned. This woman was, to put it mildly, "hot." And, if any man touched, he might well get burned with raging flames of desire.

Channa possessed a sophisticated type beauty that was manifested in her precise diction, articulate manner, ramrod straight posture and regal bearing. This was a woman who exuded self-confidence like Michael Jordan on a basketball court. You just felt that this woman, like Michael, could always hit that last shot to win the game. Yes, Channa was a real winner.

Like Ingrid, she usually wore her long dark brown hair in a pony tail, and it was usually pulled to one side and dangled on her front left shoulder, covering her generous left breast, which was shaped like what Lynton always called a tear drop, jokingly saying men were always shedding tears of desire when they noticed how provocatively they seemed to protrude from her taunt body, projecting outward like two small mountain peaks that stood boldly in the sky.

LYNTON AND THE VAMPIRE
AT TAGAYTAY MANOR NEAR THE VOLCANO
THAT SPEWED SORROW RATHER THAN LAVA

A touch of sophistication was also added by the large brown rimmed glasses that she usually wore. They seemed to magnify what could only be described as penetratingly dark brown bedroom eyes that twinkled with a hint of mischievous intent. Her lips were thick and succulent, seemingly begging to be kissed. Put all that provocative allure on a taunt 5:7 inch brown frame that tapered onto luscious, long, magnificently shaped legs and you had a human stick of female dynamite that could explode with heart pounding sexiness. This woman was, like Ingrid, way too hot to handle without getting burned, and believe me; many men had suffered third degrees burns trying to put out a raging fire of desire.

Now, contrasted with Ingrid and Channa was sweet, demure, almost pixie-like Lynton, whose penchant for being a sweet woman made her far more than the 5:2 dynamo of raw sexuality that made men's hearts palpitate with desire. The most alluring part of her entire body was an incredible smile that could light up a dark room with its sparkling intensity. It would slowly and provocatively sweep across her lips from the left side of her mouth until it gradually exposed gleaming white teeth that glistened like diamonds lighting the way to ecstasy for any man lucky enough to wrap his arms around a bronzed frame that was as taut as an archer's bow when it is pulled back ready send an arrow flying through the air. Years of professional dancing and a short stint as a star professional volleyball player had made her body a living, breathing, sinewy temple of palpitating desirous beauty that sent men's minds spinning with crazed passionate rapacious libido induced lust for just one touch of her soft, silky smooth, ductile skin.

The only problem for men was her complete devotion to her boyfriend Wayne who had won her heart with his flowery language that made her swoon with love for the first boyfriend to look beyond her physical beauty and see the inner beauty that sparkled like a great beacon on the shore guiding a ship to safe harbour. Wayne was always safe in her arms, and she could feel safe in his arms, knowing the intensity of his love.

Leonardo Da Vinci spent a lifetime trying to paint the perfect physical specimen of a woman. Scientists and mathematicians have puzzled for centuries over what makes one, while cosmetic surgeons have amassed fortunes striving to create one. And what of Lynton Viñas? Well, she simply is the perfect physical creation of a woman. She is blessed with the perfect face. It matches an international blueprint for the optimum ratio between eyes, mouth, forehead and chin, endowing her with perfect proportions. She needed no makeup as her flawless skin represented complete perfection.

She had large, dark, penetrating eyes that sparkled with a hint of playful mischievous intent. Her flat Asian nose had a small hint of a mole on its left side that did not mar her beauty, but rather enhanced it. As mentioned previously, that incredible smile could shine the light of heaven on the lowest of creatures and brighten the darkest of nights. There was no weapon in her feminine armoury to which men were as vulnerable as they were to her smile. That disarming smile could melt the hardest of hearts.

Her long, slightly curly hair had that just mussed look, as if she had been in the arms of a virile lover who had brought her great pleasure. Her breasts were small but perky, seeming to sway proactively under her blouse like a gentle wave rolling into shore undulating as it dissipated on the soft sand. Her midriff was slightly pouched, not fat, but just protruding enough to add to her magnificent form. Her tiny waistline accentuated hips that swayed provocatively from side to side as she moved about as gracefully as a gazelle on an open plain. Her thighs were fibrously firm, hard and sturdily muscular, and seemed to beg for the soft touch of a virile man. Her calves were athletically firm, strong, taunt, brawny and vigorously hard as they formed a perfect adjunct to her thighs. Ankles on her were not mere flesh and bone, but, rather, when she stood still or moved they were like buttercups of desire that glistened so desirously that men would sigh when they gazed upon them.

Finally, there was her shapely derriere, which according to her boyfriend Wayne made her look as good going as she did coming. The cheeks were shaped like two ripe cantaloupes, and the way she jiggled with each slow, measured stride made it sway ever so gently from side to side, as it raised and lowered like a ship bounding on waves in the open sea. Up, down, up, down, up and down...................

LYNTON AND THE VAMPIRE
AT TAGAYTAY MANOR NEAR THE VOLCANO
THAT SPEWED SORROW RATHER THAN LAVA

Still, her real beauty lay within an independent spirit that was free to soar with the eagles. She was a woman who knew that if you followed the crowd you will usually get no further than the crowd. Consequently, she was not afraid to walk alone and answer the call of a different drummer who was playing a different melody than the one proscribed by a society that was bound by tradition that had been propagandized to people so they would be brainwashed into following a code that would forever trap them in servitude. She knew that walking alone; not following tradition would take her to places she never dreamed possible.

This 5:2, diminutive, soft spoken, painstakingly polite, woman was as regal looking as a queen sitting on a throne, but her heart was as breakable as a porcelain angel, about to teeter and fall. She rarely cried, but she did often develop moistened eyes because she feared what could happen, but the tears were reserved for "why" something beautiful did not happen. She longed for a world devoid of injustice and evil intent. She saw things as they were and asked why they could not be better. She longed for fairness in a world where the very nature of the economic system dictated unfairness.

LYNTON AND THE VAMPIRE
AT TAGAYTAY MANOR NEAR THE VOLCANO
THAT SPEWED SORROW RATHER THAN LAVA

Lynton was like fresh water in an unspoiled, pristine stream that flowed clean and pure. She was pure of thought, action and deeds. She was at ease in the great waters of life. That is what made her body more than a sexual object. She embraced the real beauty of body that melded with spirit and built a temple of fairness and justness that made her glow with a celestial light that shone with wisdom, promise and hope.

Now, her friends Channa and Ingrid on this night, as they prepared for the party, were leery that she might start on one of her homilies about how to fight injustice as she had just talked to Wayne for an hour. She had always been passionate about injustice, but since meeting Wayne, she had gotten worse thought Channa and Ingrid, because Wayne was an old time revolutionary in the Che Guevara vein who simply lived for the thrill of getting people riled up to fight authority. Lynton smiled at them as they were slipping on the corsets Wayne had, at their request, brought them on his last visit. She said, "Don't worry, Wayne and I had a nice talk without any revolutionary zeal this time. I am not going to bore you with a discourse on how to overthrow the government and destroy corporate power."

LYNTON AND THE VAMPIRE
AT TAGAYTAY MANOR NEAR THE VOLCANO
THAT SPEWED SORROW RATHER THAN LAVA

Channa and Ingrid laughed as they were adjusting their corsets. Channa said, "Hey, you wearing your corset tonight? Or is it just reserved for Wayne to see you in?"

Lynton replied, "He hasn't seen me in it. I am saving it for a special time. So, no I am not wearing my corset. Anyway, you girls are putting them on the inside of your clothes. These corsets are meant to be worn on the outside. They are for flashy dress-up."

Ingrid interjected, "We know, but for tonight that might a bit much for high society in Tagaytay."

Lynton said, "Yes, I think we should all be prim and proper tonight. I don't think these will be the kind of people who show much more than a well-turned ankle."

Channa, in her most prima and proper manner, which came easy for someone so sophisticated, said as she raised her right hand mockingly in the air as if holding something delicate, "Oh, my-my, we must maintain our proper decorum among the elite of Tagaytay. I shall remove this brazen display of sexuality and toss it aside for fear that the

LYNTON AND THE VAMPIRE
AT TAGAYTAY MANOR NEAR THE VOLCANO
THAT SPEWED SORROW RATHER THAN LAVA

blue bloods of Tagaytay might be offended."

Ingrid, as she was removing her corset, said, "Yes, we must not offend those who are the crème-de-la crème of society. How thoughtless of me to even consider such a blatant display of disrespect to the moneyed class."

They all laughed, got dressed and headed toward Ligaya Drive and the Perrdonez Estate, which much to Lynton's surprise was only a short distance down the winding mountain road from the home of Lekman Lopez. As they whizzed by Tagaytay Manor, Lynton pointed it out to Channa and Ingrid. The two both felt a cold chill run up and down their spines. Ingrid, in a soft voice, almost as if she was fearful of being heard, said "There is something evil about that place."

The three girls all dressed up and ready to party!!!

LYNTON AND THE VAMPIRE
AT TAGAYTAY MANOR NEAR THE VOLCANO
THAT SPEWED SORROW RATHER THAN LAVA

CHAPTER 4

EVIL UNLEASHED

THE VAMPIRE'S BITE

Just like an angel with evil eye,
I shall come to thee silently,
Upon thy bower I'll alight,
With falling shadows of the night

With thee, my host, I'll commune,
And give thee kisses cold as the moon,
And with a serpent's moist embrace,
I'll crawl around thy resting-place.

And when the livid morning falls,
Thou'lt find alone the empty walls,
And till the evening, cold 'twill be.
I hide in my coffin no one to see.

As others with their tenderness,
Gaze upon thy life and youthfulness,
I'll reign alone with dread o'er thee.
Oh, my little bite marks are hard to see.

LYNTON AND THE VAMPIRE
AT TAGAYTAY MANOR NEAR THE VOLCANO
THAT SPEWED SORROW RATHER THAN LAVA

The Perrdonez family had moved to Tagaytay eight years before to escape the over bearing heat and humidity of Manila. Ironically, it was at exactly that time that Lekman Lopez moved into Tagaytay Manor. In fact, it was the exact same day.

Harold Perrdonez, who was now almost 30, lived a life, as the son of Patrice Perrdonez, his stepmother and Paul Perrdonez, his father, often called organized debauchery. Harold's mom had died in his third year of life, so he only knew Patrice as his mother, but he had a good-natured governess named Lettie, who had been with him more than her, and was probably more attached to him than his mother. In fact, she had stayed on long after he grew up and had become somewhat of a revered figure who simply helped out around the house when and where needed. Harold could not remember a time when her fat, benignant face was not a familiar picture in his memory. His stepmother was a native of Romania, and had been the housemaid when his real mother died. Madam Perrdonez was an austere woman and appeared to be extremely cold and calculating. On the other hand, Paul Perrdonez was gregarious and outgoing, but there seemed to be something

LYNTON AND THE VAMPIRE
AT TAGAYTAY MANOR NEAR THE VOLCANO
THAT SPEWED SORROW RATHER THAN LAVA

sinister about him, almost as if his outward gaiety hid a deep, dark family secret that he never wanted to see the light of day.

Lynton, Ingrid and Channa were all greeted politely by Paul and Patrice Perrdonez, and they were introduced to the 6 other guests, all who seemed a bit unsual as they appeared to have strange, far-away look in their eyes. However, when the girls were introduced to Harold, there appeared to be an intense interest on his part in Ingrid. In fact, when he reached out to take her hand, he held it at length as he looked intensely into her eyes. Ingrid felt a bit uncomfortable about his gaze, but she had to admit that her hormones were stirring with a frenzied excitement as it was obvious that Harold Perrdonez found her most alluring.

For those who read *Lynton Walks on Water*, it should be understandable why Ingrid wanted to be cautious about any romantic entanglements as she had been badly burned by a previous encounter with a fascinating, but ultimately deceptive man. Still, she was flattered by Harold's interest, and he made it blatantly obvious that he was interested in her as he even went so far as to rearrange the place cards that had been put on the dinning room table so that he could sit next to her during dinner.

Ingrid was asked to walk in the garden with Harold after dinner, and it was there that she learned notwithstanding his outgoing and gregarious nature that Harold's existence was a rather solitary one, as he rarely strayed far from his home, except to see their neighbour Lekman Lopez on occasion. The mention of Lopez piqued Ingrid's interest and she said, "Well, how strange, as we are all fascinated by the stories we have heard about Mr. Lopez. Can you tell me about him?"

"Tell you about him," said a surprised Harold, "why you will meet him in awhile. He could not make it to dinner tonight, but be dropping by shortly. He is our dear friend."

Somewhat shocked, Ingrid said "I know you must have heard rumours about him?"

"Of course, just silly superstitious townspeople who have nothing better to do with their lives than produce outlandish tales of vampires, goblins and ghosts. Ridiculous!"

LYNTON AND THE VAMPIRE
AT TAGAYTAY MANOR NEAR THE VOLCANO
THAT SPEWED SORROW RATHER THAN LAVA

"Well," said Ingrid with intensity. "We are here to find out the real story behind all this."

With a subdued laugh, Harold took her by the hand and said, "Enough talk of vampires, let's talk about us. I want to see more of you. How about a day trip to the volcano tomorrow?"

Ingrid, flattered that he was showing so much interest, said "Sure, why not?"

They heard the doorbell ring and Harold said, "That will be Lekman. Come, let me introduce you to him, but promise you won't desert me. He is older, but oh my, he is a fine specimen of a man and women do swoon in his presence."

Ingrid took his arm as they went back toward the house and very softly whispered, "No one could be more charming than you."

How wrong Ingrid was, because Lekman Lopez was simply the most charming man she had ever met. Even

LYNTON AND THE VAMPIRE
AT TAGAYTAY MANOR NEAR THE VOLCANO
THAT SPEWED SORROW RATHER THAN LAVA

Channa and the extremely discerning, astute, adroit, insightful Lynton were overwhelmed by the charm, poise and savoir-faire exhibited by suave Lekman Lopez.

Lekman Lopez had good looks that made both men and women almost swoon in his presence. So perfectly chiselled were his features that it was as if he had been sculpted in a studio by one of the masters of the art world. Michelangelo, Matisse, Degas, Da Vinci never put brush to canvas or moulded clay to create such a divinely handsome creature be it male or female. Lekman's epigrammatic wit, assured persona and impeccable manners only served to ingratiate him to the three women who were there to expose his nefarious intentions. "How" they all thought could this man of refinement and cultured mannerisms be what Lupe had intonated. This man might be a vampire, but so what? What woman wouldn't submit to a little nibble on the neck from such a handsome, virile looking man of about 40 who made James Bond look like an amateur at attracting women? As the night wore on, it was obvious by the way all the women there fawned over him that this was no ordinary man. Yet, while all the others were being wowed by his charm and wit, Lynton could not help but notice something extremely unusual about his eyes. They seemed to be focused on each person as he spoke to them almost as if he was stupefying the individual with a hypnotic stare that completely captivated and mesmerized them. All present seemed to hang on very word he said.

There were also his teeth, which were perfectly straight and glistening white. However, his upper canine incisors were pointed like the fangs of a wolf. In fact, never had Lynton seen such pronounced incisors on a human. Still, they did not detract from his handsomeness, nor, she thought, did it indicate he was a vampire. "Yeah" Lynton laughingly whispered to herself. "He was no vampire – werewolf maybe but definitely no vampire."

All who were gathered there were rich, except for Lynton. Only Channa and Ingrid, along with Lynton, seemed appalled as the conversation moved toward how the poor were a drain on society and needed to be corralled into barrios where their filth and poverty could be isolated from the upper classes. The arrogance of those present was beginning to crate on the three girls who were champions for the downtrodden and forgotten.

LYNTON AND THE VAMPIRE
AT TAGAYTAY MANOR NEAR THE VOLCANO
THAT SPEWED SORROW RATHER THAN LAVA

Lekman looked over in a disarming fashion at Lynton, his mesmerizingly hypnotic eyes boring in like a beacon, and said, "You are laughing inside young lady. Pray tell us what is tickling your insides so that we may share in your laughter?

Lynton, a bit discombobulated at his perceptiveness, replied, "Oh, nothing, I was just remembering something my boyfriend Wayne once said when giving a speech at a Socialist Workers' Party gathering."

Lekman, who seemed to know that was not what she was really thinking, pressed on. "So, we have the girlfriend of a wild-eyed revolutionary with us tonight. Please share what he said with us my dear Lynton. We are all aware your boyfriend is the writer, Wayne Frye, perhaps he offered you a wise ditty of observational exactitude that will dazzle us with its perceptiveness and insight."

There was something condescending and dismissive of Wayne that made Lynton instantly dislike Lekman. She replied, "Oh, you were just disparaging the poor whom you see as leeches wanting a handout. It just made me think of what Wayne said in his speech at the convention. He said, 'If you love wealth greater than liberty, the tranquility of servitude greater than the animating contest for freedom, then accept your fate without protest. Crouch down in subservience to the powerful and wealthy and lick the hand that you think feeds you, but if you reject your own slavery, join me in the pursuit of economic justice.' That's all, just thinking about his love of the common man and his compassion for his plight. He nor I, and I believe I can include Ingrid and Channa, have any use for people who blame the poor for being poor. I agree that they accept their plight willingly, and add to their problems by having children they cannot afford who will just be more low wage workers to fuel the fires of the capitalists who enslave them, but they are better people than those who think their wealth makes them somehow special."

Lynton then looked over at Channa and Ingrid who sat stunned at the turn of events, as she said, "Goodnight, and thanks for having me."

Channa and Ingrid got up instantly and in unison said, "Yeah, we're outta here. Goodnight."

LYNTON AND THE VAMPIRE
AT TAGAYTAY MANOR NEAR THE VOLCANO
THAT SPEWED SORROW RATHER THAN LAVA

Lynton, proud of her two friends, smiled as she moved toward the door, but behind them Lekman looked at Paul and Patrice and nodded as he said, "foolish young ladies who know not where they are treading."

Harold, running to Ingrid's side said, "I agree with you. Please do not think me like them."

Ingrid smiled as she said, "Prove it. Take me to lunch tomorrow at the Taal Hotel. We'll see."

He smiled and said, as he opened the door for the girls, "see you tomorrow at noon – Taal Hotel."

Now Ingrid knows how to manipulated men with her feminine wiles. In fact, she is so good at it that she often says to Lynton and Channa "I amaze myself. Damn, I'm good!"

The two girls gave her the assignment of finding out just how much information Harold had on Lekman Lopez. They wanted to know all the juicy details. However, they expected to get it second hand from Ingrid, so they were surprised when she called up to their room from the hotel dining room and said, "Get down her right away. I want you to hear what Harold has to say before he goes any further. He may be friends with Lekman Lopez, but he, suspects there is something not right about him, Tagaytay Manor and the relationship he has with his mom and dad. Hurry girls, I think we may be onto something here. This vampire thing may have more credence than we thought."

Channa and Lynton laughed at what she said about vampires being a credible possibility, but they did believe there might be something nefarious going on, so they went down and were cordially greeted by Harold who obligingly ordered tea for them.

So, what follows is a tale that Harold related to all three girls. There have been no embellishments. It is reproduced here exactly as it was told to the three women.

"OK, I was a precocious child, one who frankly got pretty much everything he wanted. My mother dotted on me for the short time she was alive, so I am told, as I have few recollections of her," related Harold to the girls.

LYNTON AND THE VAMPIRE
AT TAGAYTAY MANOR NEAR THE VOLCANO
THAT SPEWED SORROW RATHER THAN LAVA

As the tea was delivered, the girls sipped intermittently as Harold continued. "My governess spent more time with me than anyone else. Her name is Lettie, and she is still with us. Just does odd jobs as needed now, because I am a bit big for a governess." He smiled at his little joke and went on with his story. "The first occurrence in my existence, which produced a terrible impression upon my mind, which, in fact, never has been effaced, was one of the very earliest incidents of my life which I can recollect. Some people might think it trifling, but it has always remained seared into my mind. The nursery was a large room in the upper story of the huge home we had in Manila, with a steep tile roof. I can't have been more than three years old, when one night I awoke, and looking round the room from my bed, failed to see my governess. Neither was anyone there; and I thought myself alone. I was not frightened, for I was one of those happy children who was studiously kept in ignorance of ghost stories, of fairy tales, and of all such lore as makes us cover up our heads when the door cracks suddenly, or the darkness makes the shadow of a bed-post dance upon the wall, nearer to our faces. I was vexed and insulted at finding myself, as I conceived, neglected, and I began to whimper, preparatory to a hearty bout of roaring;

LYNTON AND THE VAMPIRE
AT TAGAYTAY MANOR NEAR THE VOLCANO
THAT SPEWED SORROW RATHER THAN LAVA

when to my surprise, I saw a solemn, but very pretty face looking at me from the side of the bed. It was that of a young lady who was kneeling, with her hands under the cover gently stroking my chest. I looked at her with wonderment, and ceased whimpering. She caressed me with her hands, and lay down beside me on the bed, and drew me towards her, smiling; I felt immediately delightfully soothed, and fell asleep again. I was wakened by a sensation as if two needles ran into my neck at the same moment, and I cried loudly. The lady looked starkly at me, with her eyes transfixed and there was a spot of blood on her teeth, and then she slipped down onto the floor, and, I thought, hid herself under my bed."

"I was frightened, and I yelled with all my might. The room was suddenly filled with all the servants. My Dad came in with Patrice by his side, who would later be my stepmom. I don't remember my mom being there for some reason. And my dad said it was all just nonsense and that we should all go about our business. Funny thing though, my governess Lettie, after everyone left, lay her hand on the bed beside me and whispered "that hollow in the bed is warm, very warm, some one did lie there"

LYNTON AND THE VAMPIRE
AT TAGAYTAY MANOR NEAR THE VOLCANO
THAT SPEWED SORROW RATHER THAN LAVA

"I remember her petting me gently on the forehead. Then, she looked down at my neck and must have noticed something, because I can remember that look of recognition on her face. I have never asked her about it, because she would never tell me anyway, as she never mentions the incident but I suspect it was two puncture wounds."

One could see in Harold's eyes that the incident had traumatized him. He continued. "I was very nervous for a long time after that and a doctor was called in because the morning after I saw that apparition I was in a state of terror, and could not bear to be left alone. In fact, I never slept in the room alone again, as at 12 I was sent away to boarding school, then to university and then here. All the while, until I was 12 and left home, my father and then Patrice would try to comfort me. It did not help, because I knew a woman had lain beside me. I knew it I tell you. I knew it."

"I remember an older man coming in with Lettie, my governess, one day. She was rather animated in telling what happened and almost instantly he did the strangest things, the absolute strangest things. "

LYNTON AND THE VAMPIRE
AT TAGAYTAY MANOR NEAR THE VOLCANO
THAT SPEWED SORROW RATHER THAN LAVA

Harold paused for awhile, and Ingrid, enthralled with his story almost shouted, "What things? What? Go on."

"He hung a garland of garlic above the entrance to my room from the balcony, and he put up a crucifix over my bed. We were never a religious family, just the opposite, in fact. My dad had a fit and demanded the crucifix be removed. Well, it was in a way. Lettie removed it from the wall, but placed it very discreetly under my bed, tucked it back under the mattress. Patrice had a fit about the smell of the garlic, so it was removed, too. Of course, Lettie could not replace that for fear they would smell it and she might be fired."

"There was a white-haired old man used to visit Lettie, and they would prey with me, prey secretly, because she was fearful Patrice and my dad might find out. What were the words she uttered with him? Let me think."

Harold seemed to ponder for awhile, staring down at his tea and then said with vigour. "Yeah, it was – *be not afraid of the children of the night. It is they who should fear you and the God that protects you with the sign of the cross.*"

LYNTON AND THE VAMPIRE
AT TAGAYTAY MANOR NEAR THE VOLCANO
THAT SPEWED SORROW RATHER THAN LAVA

Suddenly, the floor began to shake under them and a loud rumbling noise could be heard in the distance. They looked out the window at the beautiful, serene lake and in the middle was the mighty Taal Volcano with steam rising precipitously from its dome. None in the room were frightened, as the volcano had rumbled to life often without erupting, but this was particularly distressing, not because of the fear of eruption, but because of the whining, almost sorrowful sound it was making. It was as if it was weeping, weeping like a mourning mother who had lost a child. It was not giving off steam from deep within the earth. It was spewing sorrow rather than lava. Everyone in the room looked about at one another; some with tears in their eyes so disconsolate was the sound.

The four of them got up. Harold paid the bill and they walked outside and stood on the veranda, leaning against a railing, just staring in the distance as the whining noise continued. Lynton turned to Harold and said, "Something unexplainable is happening here, something beyond our realm of understanding, but nature knows." Then she looked at Channa and Ingrid, continuing. "There is evil about to be unleashed here in Tagaytay."

LYNTON AND THE VAMPIRE
AT TAGAYTAY MANOR NEAR THE VOLCANO
THAT SPEWED SORROW RATHER THAN LAVA

CHAPTER 5

SOMETHING TERRIBLY EVIL

The moon is full and shining.
It fills the lost with delight.
It is time for them to go hunting.
These children of the night.

Listen to them mournfully calling.
The night is clear and still,
And nature sits with bated breath,
As they prowl, looking for the kill.

The mystery of their evil song
Will fill many hearts with dread.
As their wings flap in the air,
They come to take you from your bed.

And these children have no virtue,
Betraying all with a crimson bite.
If you survive, you must now join them,
These children of the night.

Come join in their evil songs
They render to the moon.
Be part of the ancient ritual
And dance to the devil's tune.

For they are Satan's children,
Who run from the light,
Delighting in the darkness,
These children of the night.

LYNTON AND THE VAMPIRE
AT TAGAYTAY MANOR NEAR THE VOLCANO
THAT SPEWED SORROW RATHER THAN LAVA

Now, I am not one to believe in anything I cannot see with my own eyes. However, it has been confirmed by many that the constant rumbling of Taal was always accompanied by a sorrowful moaning sound for the next few days. Many people left the city in fear that a catastrophe was about to occur. Yet, no lava had flowed nor had any ash been dispersed.

Channa, Ingrid and Lynton were determined to stay and try to get to the bottom of the mystery of Tagaytay Manor. They had met Lekman Lopez, and although dazzled by his looks, they were not impressed with his manner.

Their quest was going to become embroiled in what would be quite a mystery for the little town. Lupe contacted Lynton and related the following story: *Two nights after the dinner party, it appears that Lupe was walking to catch the Jeepney to work when Diane Rodriquez stepped from behind a bush and said, "Come with me. You have been selected." When Lupe refused to go, suddenly Diane seemed to almost hiss like a wild animal, and her eyes became fiery red. Only the arrival of the Jeepney kept Lupe from what she thought would have been certain death.*

LYNTON AND THE VAMPIRE
AT TAGAYTAY MANOR NEAR THE VOLCANO
THAT SPEWED SORROW RATHER THAN LAVA

Now, the reason why this story has particular relevance is that the very next morning, Diane Rodriquez's body was found on the roadside near Lupe's home. Her neck had been ripped open and it appeared a wild animal had actually eaten some of her flesh. Lynton, encouraged Lupe not to share the story with police, as it would needlessly get her embroiled in the investigation, and might even point an accusatory finger at her. The strange occurrence would be beyond the realm of belief on the part of the police anyway. Lupe agreed and even confessed that she had not even shared the information with her husband. Lynton thought to herself, what good would it do to share it with a chain-smoking jerk that would probably be too engrossed watching television to listen anyway.

There was a frenzied buzz among citizens, but the police simply said that it was a wild animal attack, probably a rabid dog, and that the populace should be very careful when stray dogs were around. Thus, first blood in Tagaytay had been drawn. With typical inefficiency the police in Tagaytay were unaware that neighbouring villages, for eight years, almost monthly had been experiencing what were assumed to be attacks by rabid dogs.

LYNTON AND THE VAMPIRE
AT TAGAYTAY MANOR NEAR THE VOLCANO
THAT SPEWED SORROW RATHER THAN LAVA

While all this was going on, Ingrid and Harold continued to see each other, much to the chagrin of Harold's parents, who had taken an intense disliking to all three girls after the night they left in a huff over the arrogance of Lekman Lopez. Ingrid was actually learning much about Lekman Lopez through Harold and she willingly shared the information with Channa and Lynton.

It appeared that Lekman had actually known Patrice Perrdonez back in Romania many years before she came to be a servant in the Perrdonez household, and eventually Paul's wife after the death of his first wife. Harold had been encouraged by his parents to befriend Lekman, and was told that on his 30 birthday he would be given a great opportunity to be part of a grand adventure that would lead him to riches that he never imagined possible. He was never given any details, just told that Lekman was a man with the key to an unlimited future where his wildest dreams could be realized.

Now, Lynton, not one to believe in superstition, was still a woman who believed that you should never go into battle without knowledge of your enemy. For that reason, she and

LYNTON AND THE VAMPIRE
AT TAGAYTAY MANOR NEAR THE VOLCANO
THAT SPEWED SORROW RATHER THAN LAVA

Channa went all the way to Quezon City to talk to Professor Marion Rodriquez while Ingrid spent the day with Harold. Professor Rodriquez was an expert on ancient superstitions, which, of course, included vampires.

The professor was a short, chubby man with a thick head of hair that looked as if it had been in a hurricane and never seen a comb. Infatuated with the two beautiful women, he was a virtual fountain of information, and it flowed from him like a machine gun spitting out information in rapid fire.

What follows is the summation of what the professor shared: Only a vampire can create another vampire, so logic tells us that the history of vampires begins with a single vampire who created the others. Much like the chicken-and-the-egg argument, we had little insight into how the first vampire came about until recently. Logically, if there was no vampire to make the first vampire, how was the first vampire made? The answer lies in the Scriptures of Delphi, specifically in the collection of writings known as *The Vampire Bible*. This book has been passed down through the ages by scholars.

LYNTON AND THE VAMPIRE
AT TAGAYTAY MANOR NEAR THE VOLCANO
THAT SPEWED SORROW RATHER THAN LAVA

The first vampire started out as not a vampire at all, but as a human man named Ambrogio. He was an Italian-born adventurer who fate brought to Delphi, in Greece. A series of blessings and curses transformed this young man into history's first vampire. Specifically, it began with the sun god Apollo, who in a fit of rage cursed Ambrogio so that his skin would burn should it ever touch sunlight again. Ambrogio's bad luck followed when he ended up gambling away his soul to the god of the underworld, Hades. The next curse came via Apollo's sister Artemis, the goddess of the moon and hunting, who made it so that Ambrogio's skin would burn if he touched silver. This silver was later transposed to a sliver bullet to kill werewolves which, of course, is a whole other legend in itself. The blessings came soon after when Artemis, taking pity on the poor young man, gave him the gift of immortality. He would carry his curses - his skin burning by sunlight or silver, but he would live forever in his current form. Blood-sucking from humans was not originally necessary for survival, but developed later on as the need for nourishment became more pronounced. Ambrogio hunted swans and used their blood originally for sustenance. No one knows why it had to be the blood of swans originally.

LYNTON AND THE VAMPIRE
AT TAGAYTAY MANOR NEAR THE VOLCANO
THAT SPEWED SORROW RATHER THAN LAVA

Ambrogio later moved back to Italy, where he became a full-fledged vampire. Legend traces him to the city of Florence, where he created the first Vampire Clan by biting others in the neck slowly over a period of time and transforming them into vampires.

Little is known about this clan, other than they were most likely willing volunteers - humans who wanted power and immortality, and were willing to trade their souls for it. It was believed that the curse would continue for any vampire where their souls would remain in the Underworld.

From what is known of the history of vampires, the clan grew in size and strength, until infighting created something of a "civil war" within the clan, and many vampires left to form their own clans. What happened to Ambrogio and those who stayed with him is largely unknown, though many believe that he still lives today; although legend tells that he eventually made his way to mountains of Transylvania in Romania to escape the wrath of the Catholic Church in Italy which had launched a crusade against vampires around the time of the Great Inquisition.

LYNTON AND THE VAMPIRE
AT TAGAYTAY MANOR NEAR THE VOLCANO
THAT SPEWED SORROW RATHER THAN LAVA

How vampires got to the point of having to rest in their coffins with some of their homeland's earth around it was simply not known. Apparently, it developed as a result of the presumed death of a vampire or a clan of vampires and someone unearthed them after burial. From that point on, they needed the safety of a coffin in the daytime.

How they escape from their graves and return to them for certain hours every day, without displacing the clay or leaving any trace of disturbance in the state of the coffin or the cerements, has always been admitted to be utterly inexplicable. Of course, in some cases they have henchmen who maintain their coffin in a crept or vault, assisting the vampire in its nightly rise from the dead. The amphibious existence of the vampire is sustained by daily renewed slumber in the grave. Its horrible lust for living blood supplies the vigour of its waking existence. The vampire is prone to be fascinated with an engrossing vehemence, resembling the passion of love, by particular persons. In pursuit of these it will exercise inexhaustible patience and stratagem, for access to a particular object may be obstructed in a hundred ways. It will never desist until it has satiated its passion, and drained the very life of its coveted victim. But it will, in these cases, husband and protract its murderous enjoyment with the refinement of an epicure, and heighten it by the gradual approaches of an artful courtship. In these cases it seems to yearn for something like sympathy and consent. In ordinary ones it goes direct to its object, overpowers with violence and strangles and exhausts often at a single feast.

Now, at this point, it should be noted that the professor mentioned a particular name which piqued Lynton and Channa's interest immensely. He went on with a story about a family named Kabian. The head of the family was a nobleman and he was assumed to be a vampire who was answerable to his master, who was rumoured to be Ambrogio. He lived in relative anonymity. There are many journals, and other papers, written by vampire hunters who tell of trying to trace Ambrogio's whereabouts. None seem to have succeeded.

Lynton looked knowingly at Channa. They were two sceptical women, but they had dealt with the supernatural before and learned that there is some fact in all legends. But no, Lekman Lopez could not be Ambrogio.

LYNTON AND THE VAMPIRE
AT TAGAYTAY MANOR NEAR THE VOLCANO
THAT SPEWED SORROW RATHER THAN LAVA

They thanked the professor, and armed with some fundamental knowledge set out to see if they could help Lupe and perhaps solve the mystery of Lekman Lopez and Tagaytay Manor.

While Channa and Lynton were visiting the professor, Ingrid was enjoying a day with Harold Perrdonez. Although filled with the usual romantic interludes, Ingrid could not resist trying to find out more about the family's connection with Lekman Lopez. As they stood by the observation deck railing in the Taal Amusement Park staring down at the volcano, Ingrid said, "Harold, so tell me about your stepmother's connection to Lekman Lopez."

"Nothing much to tell, Patrice apparently knew his servant Quinton Sagrando back in Romania. He introduced Patrice to my real mother, whom he had once met when she was visiting Transylvania as a young unmarried woman. I think they had maybe even been lovers before she married my dad. Anyway, I was about to be born, so my mom took her on as sort of a helper. She was fairly good to me, always has been. For some reason though I must admit to always having been a bit frighten of her."

LYNTON AND THE VAMPIRE
AT TAGAYTAY MANOR NEAR THE VOLCANO
THAT SPEWED SORROW RATHER THAN LAVA

Ingrid, her curiosity aroused, ask, "Why would you be frightened by her?"

"I don't know Ingrid, just a few things that have happened over the years. You remember what happened to me as a child that night in my bedroom?"

Ingrid, intensely interested now, and trying to glean information that would be beneficial to share with Lynton and Channa, said "Yes. It was very frightening indeed."

Well, that night I remember, after everyone else had left, when she stayed in the room, when my governess drifted off to sleep she bent over me and softly whispered, "It's OK Harold. Everything will be clear to you in your 30th year. Don't be afraid, go to sleep now and embrace the children of the night. It is unfortunate your visit with one of them was interrupted. Just remember that Jesus began his ministry at 30, and you will begin immortality at 30 my sweet boy."

"And why was that so frightful? Was it what she said or the way she said it?"

LYNTON AND THE VAMPIRE
AT TAGAYTAY MANOR NEAR THE VOLCANO
THAT SPEWED SORROW RATHER THAN LAVA

"It was both Ingrid," said a pensive Harold, who continued his discourse. "It was what she said, as if there was something momentous going to happen on my 30th birthday, which, by the way, is only a few weeks away. Yet, it was something that gave me a fright, made me shiver with fear because of the way she whispered it, so sinister it was."

Ingrid, fascinated asked, "And what of that phrase she used – *children of the night?*"

"I once asked her about that. She looked at me with anger and said, 'Don't mention that again. One day you will know what I meant, but it is not to be discussed now. I should not have said it. All will be clear to you one day dear boy. Remember, Jesus did not start his ministry until he was 30. You will start your ministry of the night then.' There was something frightening about the way she said *ministry of the night*. I am actually scared of turning 30 Ingrid. I feel great trepidation about my impending birthday. A few days ago Lekman said to me that he and my mother were planning a grand party for me, but that it would be a private affair to be held at Tagaytay Manor."

LYNTON AND THE VAMPIRE
AT TAGAYTAY MANOR NEAR THE VOLCANO
THAT SPEWED SORROW RATHER THAN LAVA

Ingrid placed her left hand on Harold's right arm and said sympathetically, "Do not worry Harold. You tell Lekman that you are spending your birthday with me, Lynton and Channa. We'll all put our sexy corsets on and let you escort us to Tagaytay's finest club, where you can be the envy of all men when they see you with three beautiful, gorgeous, alluring, captivating women. You lucky boy, you!"

They laughed and began to stroll down the walkway, back to the main park. They did not notice that trailing behind them was a solitary figure in black as the sun had sat while they were talking. There was a red tint on the distant horizon caused by the setting sun as the figure moved clandestinely out of sight, seeming to hide from the slight rays of the sun that were still dancing about. It was as if the sun's small, almost indistinguishable rays were causing the figure pain and he had to hide periodically to escape from the slight light that was left from the setting sun.

The two enjoyed a wonderful evening, and at 10:00 PM, Harold left Ingrid at her hotel room, where she impatiently waited for Lynton and Channa's return.

LYNTON AND THE VAMPIRE
AT TAGAYTAY MANOR NEAR THE VOLCANO
THAT SPEWED SORROW RATHER THAN LAVA

Discussing what the professor had shared with them, Lynton and Channa were excited about sharing the information with Ingrid, who, being less cerebral then they were, was able to cut through the claptrap of intellectualism to the core of things. Hers was a wise counsel, because she possessed the ability to decipher things in a way that got right to the crux of the matter. And her direct manner made you know exactly what she thought without any reservations or caveats.

While Channa, with her usual gear shifting precision, was taking one of her notorious shortcuts, Ingrid decided to take a stroll on the hotel veranda downstairs. As she leisurely meandered about, casting an eye down on the volcano that was venting some steam, she was particularly taken with the rumbling sound it was emitting. It sounded almost like a mournful whine. Yes, it sounded as if the volcano was not spewing lava but sorrow, and it reminded Ingrid of the lover she had lost in the nearby village of Taal, where she and her two friends had exposed a charlatan, and where Lynton had literally walked on water. Oh, she wanted to forget Bradley, but it was difficult to forget one who had captured your heart, then betrayed you.

LYNTON AND THE VAMPIRE
AT TAGAYTAY MANOR NEAR THE VOLCANO
THAT SPEWED SORROW RATHER THAN LAVA

She recalled a poem from her youth that seemed apropos as the volcano rumbled its discontent. The sorrowful moan of the volcano made her lament her lost love, the one whom she thought perfect until reality sat in. Now, she knew that he was gone and would return to her nevermore, just as the poem had said about the poet's lover. Bradley was gone forever. Could Harold make her forget? Could she trust Harold, or was he, like Bradley, the shadow of a demon hanging over her lonely, still grieving soul that longed for love. She starting reciting the poem adjusting the words to her unique situation, and all the while, as she continued her midnight stroll, she felt an uneasiness, a weariness. There was an unseen presence there with her as a solitary figure moved gracefully and stealthily in the shadows. She felt the presence and a chill overwhelmed her body. She actually shivered.

FRIGHT NIGHT AT THE TAAL HOTEL

Once upon a midnight dreary,
while she pondered weak and weary,
suddenly there came a tapping from behind,
some one gently rapping, rapping at her sombre mind.
Could it be someone with malevolent intent?

LYNTON AND THE VAMPIRE
AT TAGAYTAY MANOR NEAR THE VOLCANO
THAT SPEWED SORROW RATHER THAN LAVA

It was such a black night,

And there was a ghostly presence in the shadows

as vainly she had sought to borrow sanity.

She was lamenting her lost love

who had left her when push came to shove.

And the uncertain rumbling of the volcano's curtain

filled her with fantastic terrors never felt before.

She stood still, hearing the beating of her heart.

Who is this visitor of the mind?

Can it be a demon unkind?

"Sir," she shouted and turned.

The slight rapping of a cane stopped.

She stood in silence staring into the blackness.

The shadows danced in the darkness with despair.

She stood there this lady so fair.

Deep into that darkness peering,

she was still, quiet and fearing.

Doubting, dreaming dreams of demons in the dark.

But the silence was unbroken,

and the darkness gave her no token.

J. WAYNE FRYE 94

LYNTON AND THE VAMPIRE
AT TAGAYTAY MANOR NEAR THE VOLCANO
THAT SPEWED SORROW RATHER THAN LAVA

Back toward the volcano turning,

all her soul began burning,

Soon again she heard a tapping louder than before.

"Surely," said she, "surely there is something there.

Can it be a demon from fanciful lore?"

Suddenly emerging from the darkness with a flutter,

yes, it was like the flutter of a bat's wings,

stood tall, ram-rod straight Lekman Lopez,

his eyes honed in on her and he says,

"Listen to the volcano as a sweet melody it sings."

Seemingly extreme obeisance made he;

but not a minute stopped or tarried he;

but, with mien of lord on high,

perched above Ingrid he moved forward

and she swooned as in his arms she wanted to lie.

There was not any need for smiling,

as in his cold red eyes she saw the grave.

He swept her into his arms as he was craven.

His sharp teeth glistened in the moonlight.

How he desired the neck of the sweet young maiden.

J. WAYNE FRYE   95

LYNTON AND THE VAMPIRE
AT TAGAYTAY MANOR NEAR THE VOLCANO
THAT SPEWED SORROW RATHER THAN LAVA

Lekman Lopez whispered softly,
"Relax as it will not hurt.
Listen to the lonely, sorrowful rumble of Taal.
Ah, its sweet sorrow is music to my ears.
After my bite you shall have no fears."

His soul in those words he did outpour.
Nothing further did he utter,
but Ingrid heard a light flutter,
as his black cloak flapped in the breeze,
and she fell into his arms with ease.

Startled at the stillness as no words were aptly spoken,
she was hypnotically willing to court disaster
in the arms of he who was now her master.
Ill-will for blood, he so proudly bore
for he had long ago closed heaven's door.

Lekman Lopez was most beguiling,
his sad soul was smiling.
Into his arms Ingrid was slowly sinking,
but he desired blood from this sweet miss,
sighing in ecstasy waiting for the kiss.

LYNTON AND THE VAMPIRE
AT TAGAYTAY MANOR NEAR THE VOLCANO
THAT SPEWED SORROW RATHER THAN LAVA

So enthralled she did not engage in guessing,

for no syllable was expressing.

This bat of a man whose fiery eyes now burned

into her wilting soul's core;

lust for blood was what he had learned.

Then, the air grew denser,

perfumed from an unseen censor.

Swung by from heaven, two angels appeared.

"Evil wretch," cried Lynton.

"Deplorable heathen," shouted Channa.

Lekman turned from his prey,

his eyes burning with hate.

Smiling, he whispered his evil.

"No one can avoid their fate.

Time will come when you rue this day".

"Thing of evil," said Lynton.

Channa, her precise diction not wavering, cried,

"Your evil we will bury where you lie."

Disconsolate, yet completely undaunted,

Lekman with words the women assaulted.

LYNTON AND THE VAMPIRE
AT TAGAYTAY MANOR NEAR THE VOLCANO
THAT SPEWED SORROW RATHER THAN LAVA

"I have wandered this earth for thousands of years.

People like you cause the children of the night no fears.

Even heaven bends before me.

No one will believe what you say

you have seen on this dark day."

"Demon!" said Lynton, "thing of evil!"

"This is a woman we adore.

From her, there shall be no blood.

We have defeated demons before.

We know how to close the devil's door."

Lekman, his eyes like smouldering embers, said

"Be careful my beauties when you mess with the undead.

You are fair and radiant maidens

but you are no match for me.

Just wait. Just wait and you will see."

"Be that word our sign of parting fiend!" shrieked Lynton

"Get thee back into hell from whince you came.

We place no credence in the lies you have spoken!

Leave us and our souls will stay unbroken!

We seek solace not glory or fame."

LYNTON AND THE VAMPIRE
AT TAGAYTAY MANOR NEAR THE VOLCANO
THAT SPEWED SORROW RATHER THAN LAVA

And Lekman, never flitting,

still was smiling, yes still smiling,

as if dreaming a demon's dream

sitting by the devil's stream

plotting about their defiling.

The moonlight throws his shadow on the ground,

and these girls souls are easily found.

He turns to walk away as they embrace,

As together they know any evil they can face.

Then the volcano makes that loathsome sound.

In an instance they hear the flutter of wings.

They look skyward at the full moon hanging high,

and there fluttering across it eerily in the sky

is a giant bat whose image blackens the night

and fills all who gaze upon it with fright.

These three had experience battling demons before, both supernatural and natural (human beings). Yet, so frightened were they that they slept with the lights on. Ingrid kept looking in the mirror for days at her neck to make sure there were no bite marks.

LYNTON AND THE VAMPIRE
AT TAGAYTAY MANOR NEAR THE VOLCANO
THAT SPEWED SORROW RATHER THAN LAVA

As they pondered their next step, Harold continued his courting of Ingrid, and when she told him of the strange occurrence that night on the veranda of Taal Hotel, he just laughed and said that obviously she, as well as Lynton and Channa, had simply had too much to drink.

Finally, Ingrid said, "Harold, I rarely drink, and when I do, it is never to excess. My friends talked to a professor at the university who had some interesting insight into what is going on here. I am a religious person, so I must admit to having some superstitions, but I am not a fool. I know what I saw that night on the veranda, and after some of your experiences, maybe you should not be so doubtful. I think we all need to sit town and talk about the strange occurrences here in Tagaytay recently."

Harold wiped his forehead slowly and said, "Ingrid, I am scared. I am scared of Lekman Lopez for the first time in my life, and there is something strange about my stepmother and even my father when it comes to Lekman. It is like he has a hold on them, something that makes them cot-tow and cater to him. I don't want to admit it, but there is something evil going on here – something terribly evil."

LYNTON AND THE VAMPIRE
AT TAGAYTAY MANOR NEAR THE VOLCANO
THAT SPEWED SORROW RATHER THAN LAVA

CHAPTER 6

AMBRAGIO TRAVELELD UNDER

THE SPANISH NAME LEKMAN LOPEZ

His surrogate mother, horrific
And full of fiery blasphemy,
Cursed her non-existent God,
And exalted the evil she served.

Her adopted son in a serpent's nest entire,
In exaltation, he is the Child of Doom!
Glorified be that transient night of vain desire.
His expiation came when he emerged from the womb.

Time be not cast in a vacuum.
Degradation was a jaded result of evil intentions.
Harold cannot like a love-leaf wantonly
Consign a stunted monster to the glowing grate.

Upon she who only knows perverted love,
Is played the curded tool of Lekman Lopez.
Forsooth, the branches of the wretched tree
Rob pestilential blossoms of their might.

LYNTON AND THE VAMPIRE
AT TAGAYTAY MANOR NEAR THE VOLCANO
THAT SPEWED SORROW RATHER THAN LAVA

So thus, she giveth vent into her foaming ire,
Knowing not the statues of loving times,
As she prepares, amid flames of hell, the evil pyre,
The consecrated offerings of maternal crimes.

What is not known often hides explanations that make the pieces of a puzzle fall into place and complete the picture. Lynton, Ingrid and Channa were now on a mission to slowly and methodically place the pieces of a puzzle together, but they needed to explore the reasons behind Lekman's move to Tagaytay along with the coincidence of the Perrdonez family showing up at the same time. Though not sure, the three girls were fairly certain that there was a correlation, and once uncovered, that might provide some definitive answers.

The fact that Channa and Lynton had already accumulated fundamental knowledge about vampires from the professor was going to be a help, but the story of Ambrogio needed clarification, so Lynton called Wayne on Vancouver Island and asked him for assistance in getting more information on vampires, which elicited a laugh from him but also, because of his love and devotion, assurance to

LYNTON AND THE VAMPIRE
AT TAGAYTAY MANOR NEAR THE VOLCANO
THAT SPEWED SORROW RATHER THAN LAVA

Lynton that he would do what he could, as, although he thought the idea of vampires ridiculous, most tall tales and legends did have some basis in reality, and once historical perspective was taken into consideration there were often plausible explanations to things. He knew of a professor at the University of British Columbia who specialized in the study of vampire legends, and he would explore various avenues with him that might be of assistance.

Now, if ever there was a sceptic, it was Wayne, a man who was an idealist who believed that the human condition was deplorable when there was so much abundance in the world, but that most of the abundance was reserved for the top 1% while the rest of humanity had to toil in obscurity to serve the interests of the few. Wayne was a dying breed, an anachronism in a modern world where greed was exalted as an enviable trait to promote capitalism and the corporate culture that had hijacked a good idea and sold it to a gullible public that actually believed the "average guy" could compete with giant corporations in the marketplace. Wayne saw through the propaganda and longed for fairness and justice in a world where it was in incredibly short supply.

LYNTON AND THE VAMPIRE
AT TAGAYTAY MANOR NEAR THE VOLCANO
THAT SPEWED SORROW RATHER THAN LAVA

This penchant for justice, and love of the common man was what had originally endeared Wayne to Lynton, making her fall in love with him the very first time she met him when she was on a tour of British Columbia appearing in nightclubs there with Channa and Ingrid. He was different from other men she had met, who were more interested in her beauty and sex appeal than in her depth of character. Wayne had jokingly told her, "Sex is a bonus in a relationship, not the primary reason for it. You can't have sex 24 hours a day, so there better be something more substantial to a relationship than sex." Of course, she had often told Wayne after they became lovers, "You didn't lie to me about sex, you can't do it 24 hours a day, but with you, there is a concentrated effort to make it at least 23 hours a day!"

Long distance relationships can be tough, but in their case, the nature of Wayne's profession as a writer made it possible for him to spend a lot of time with her in the Philippines, and her career as an entertainer provided her ample free time to visit him in Canada. They appeared to be ideally suited for one another, and their devotion to each other made many of their friends envious of their love.

LYNTON AND THE VAMPIRE
AT TAGAYTAY MANOR NEAR THE VOLCANO
THAT SPEWED SORROW RATHER THAN LAVA

Wayne had left the USA in 2003 to escape what he termed the pervasive lunacy that had taken over the country when George Bush was appointed President by the Supreme Court which was followed by 9/11 hysteria. As he walked onto the ferry on Vancouver Island, he looked about and breathed in the crisp, clean air, looked out at all the pristine islands in the distance and sighed contently, realizing that he had left behind a place where greed seemed to be at the core of everything. He was in a country where healthcare was a right rather than a privilege, where government served as a buffer to protect citizens from corporate power, where poverty existed but where government saw to it that no one went without, where the military was never used as a means to subjugate other nations, where religion was not allowed to dictate public policy, where the tax system took a fair amount from the rich to help the poor rather than taking from the poor to help the rich, and above all, he saw his life transformed by freeing himself from the propaganda that was used to make people believe they were free, when in fact, they were wearing shackles that bound them to an idea that was not practiced in reality. Yes, Wayne was free, genuinely free for the first time in his life. Real freedom felt so good.

LYNTON AND THE VAMPIRE
AT TAGAYTAY MANOR NEAR THE VOLCANO
THAT SPEWED SORROW RATHER THAN LAVA

Meanwhile, back in Tagaytay, Lynton, Ingrid and Channa were making their way to Lupe's home to go back over, in detail, everything she saw that night at Tagaytay Manor. As was customary, Lupe's husband, Richie, was too engrossed in television and his cigarette puffing to offer anything besides a cursory wave of the hand when Lupe introduced Channa and Ingrid. Watching him made all three girls feel sorry for Lupe, who obviously was the sole support for the family, and she received no help or acknowledgement from a disinterested husband who was more married to the television than to Lupe.

Lynton could not resist raising her voice so Richie could hear her over the roar of the television. "Lupe, you keep a very clean house, and you work so hard. You are to be complimented for your devotion as a mother and wife."

She could tell that Richie heard the words, as he shifted in his seat a bit and actually placed his cigarette down in a butt-filled ashtray on the coffee table where he had his feet propped up. He was listening, and Lynton could not resist letting him know that Lupe deserved some respect and appreciation. So, she continued with her praise. "This is the cleanest place I think I have ever been in. It must not be easy with so many children, and having to work hard every day. I am so fortunate, because when my boyfriend is here with me, while I am at work, he does the washing, cleans the house and does the grocery shopping. He realizes how hard I work and tries to show his love and appreciation in those ways. Now, there is a real man."

Lupe, almost embarrassed, because she knew what Lynton was doing, looked over at Richie as she said, "Yes, you are lucky indeed." She then gave Lynton a little wink and continued, "Appreciation is very important in a relationship. It solidifies and makes it stronger. I bet you reward him in little ways for his love don't you?"

Smiling and winking back at Lupe, Lynton said, "Of course, we women have to reward a man for his love, generosity and kindness, especially when we lie down with him at night."

Suddenly, Richie got up and started picking up the debris on the coffee table. He went over and got the broom from the corner and begin to sweep.

LYNTON AND THE VAMPIRE
AT TAGAYTAY MANOR NEAR THE VOLCANO
THAT SPEWED SORROW RATHER THAN LAVA

Lupe said, "Come, let's sit out on the stoop and talk." As they walked outside she bent over and whispered in Lynton's ear, "Thank you."

Lynton smiled and as they sat down said, "So, you are 100% positive that you saw Lekman bite Diane Rodriguez. You have no doubts?"

"I do not. I saw the blood on his teeth. I also saw the marks later on her neck. She was, well, she seemed hypnotized when I saw her there with him, and even when she confronted me at my workplace, she had a certain stare about her, almost as if she was simply repeating what she had been told to say, like she did not have a will of her own. It was so frightening, and I still shiver with fear when I think about what she said."

Channa asked, "Do you have any idea why she would have been near your house when she was killed?"

"No, there would be no reason for her to be here. If she was visiting Lekman, she would have waited for the Jeepney across from his house, not across from mine."

LYNTON AND THE VAMPIRE
AT TAGAYTAY MANOR NEAR THE VOLCANO
THAT SPEWED SORROW RATHER THAN LAVA

Ingrid offered an explanation. "Maybe she was having second thoughts about what she had said to you at work that day. Perhaps she was freeing herself from Lekman Lopez's magnetic spell."

"She could have been. We were not good friends, but did know each other as two of my children had her as a teacher a few years ago. She was a good teacher, and seemed to genuinely care about the kids. That night at the restaurant, it was not she who said, 'Bringing in that demon hunting bitch won't do you any good Lupe. Nobody can help you now. It is too late for you. Have a good evening at work.' That simply was not the Diana Rodriguez I knew – no way. She would never have talked like that, and the look she had on her face was not Diana. I tell you she was under that evil man's power. It was Lekman Lopez talking through her. I know it sounds crazy, but it was. It was. I know it."

Richie came outside carrying a bag filled with trash. He actually said "excuse me" as he walked between the girls on the steps of the porch. The change was not complete, but it was a start Lynton thought as Richie again said "excuse me" as he walked back in.

LYNTON AND THE VAMPIRE
AT TAGAYTAY MANOR NEAR THE VOLCANO
THAT SPEWED SORROW RATHER THAN LAVA

"Well, I agree that there is something deeply sinister about Lekman Lopez," said Lynton as she crossed her legs and sighed. "I am not ready to say he is a vampire, but I do know there is a connection somehow between his showing up here at almost the exact time as the Perrdonez family." Then she looked over at Ingrid as she asked the next question. "Can you tell me anything about Harold Perrdonez?"

Ingrid's eyes got a little bigger, as she waited for Lupe's answer. Lupe was very precise and measured in her response. "I don't know him at all really. Obviously, I move in a different social class than he does. However, I am acquainted with him as he comes into the restaurant from time to time and I have taken his order, and he is always cordial whenever I see him, even to the point of referring to me by name and asking how I am. He seems much nicer than the rest of the family. They are all more aloof acting than he is. He does not seem to think of himself as something special because of his economic status. I can't say that about the rest of the family. They all seem a bit arrogant, even the servants appear to think they are special just because they work for them."

LYNTON AND THE VAMPIRE
AT TAGAYTAY MANOR NEAR THE VOLCANO
THAT SPEWED SORROW RATHER THAN LAVA

"OK," said Lynton as she got up. "I have my boyfriend Wayne working on this in Canada. He is a writer and is great at ferreting out information that others can't. I am sure he will come up with something for us." She motioned for the girls to get up, and as they did Richie came out of the house with a pitcher of lemonade.

He smiled at them and said, "I thought you girls might like something cool to drink." As he handed the tray to Lupe, all four of the young women fought back laughter as Richie reached up and took his cigarette out of his mouth and tossed it away, saying, "sorry about blowing smoke in your face, filthy habit smoking. I've got to stop."

Lupe looked Lynton in the eyes, and although there were no words spoken, written on Lupe's face was the word "thanks."

Lynton, Channa and Ingrid all thanked Richie, sat down and sipped lemonade for awhile with the two. Lynton thought to herself that men were like children. They wanted to do the right thing, but you had to give them that little nudge to get them off their lazy butts.

LYNTON AND THE VAMPIRE
AT TAGAYTAY MANOR NEAR THE VOLCANO
THAT SPEWED SORROW RATHER THAN LAVA

Meanwhile, as Lynton sipped tea, Wayne was walking into the University of British Columbia office of Dr. Lorton Myron McCormack who was a man obviously immensely impressed with himself. The large type name plate on his desk made certain everyone knew he was Dr. McCormack. Wayne always felt it was inappropriate to call a person who was not an MD or a dentist a doctor. When he had his first professorship at the City University of New York, although completed, he had not yet received his Ph.D. Always a believer in never exalting oneself needlessly; he had his students call him Wayne. When word got out to his students that he had finally received the official approval of his dissertation, in class that day they said, "I suppose we will have to call you Dr. Frye now."

Wayne laughingly replied, "No one had enough respect to call me Mr. Frye before, so I see no reason to call me Dr. Frye now." They all had a good laugh, and he continued to be known as Wayne to his students. In fact, even when he was president of two universities, he insisted students call him Wayne, because he felt that you earned respect, not by titles that were so coveted by many, but by your deeds and actions which fostered reverence and veneration.

LYNTON AND THE VAMPIRE
AT TAGAYTAY MANOR NEAR THE VOLCANO
THAT SPEWED SORROW RATHER THAN LAVA

Dr. McCormack was obviously an intelligent man, but it was apparent that he relished that title doctor, as he made it a point to let Wayne know he should be referred to as Dr. McCormack when he said, "I am Dr. McCormack, very pleased to meet you Wayne."

Wayne thought respect should always be a two-way street, but Dr. McCormack's reference to him as Wayne indicated that McCormick did not harbour the same ideals. "Oh well," thought Wayne. "I have dealt with arrogant people all my life, and I usually let them know what I think of their arrogance, but not before I get what I need from them." So, Wayne settled into an overstuffed chair and prepared to work his marketing magic on Dr. McCormack.

Once called a marketing genius by the *Los Angeles Times*, Wayne knew that flattery worked magic with most people, as we all need our egos stroked. Thus he opened the conversation with praise for Dr. McCormack. "Dr. McCormack. I have read and been told that you are the premiere authority on vampire legends, and I need some information that might assist solving a mystery about vampires in the Philippines."

LYNTON AND THE VAMPIRE
AT TAGAYTAY MANOR NEAR THE VOLCANO
THAT SPEWED SORROW RATHER THAN LAVA

"Yes, I am considered the world's foremost authority on vampire legends. My books have been popular throughout the world and the reviews have been exemplary I might add."

It was all Wayne could do to hold back his desire to lower the proverbial boom on the arrogant jerk, whose books probably sold no more than a few thousand copies, but he let the bombastic educated buffoon continue to toot his own horn. "You see, as I have postulated on numerous occasions in forums, that in today's world, vampires are the stuff of mass entertainment, but they have always been thus, because the legends have been spun for generation after generation, long before mass entertainment came along. It is interesting that you mentioned the Philippines, because I have given speech at the Ambrogio Society when it met in Manila five years ago."

The mention of Ambrogio piqued Wayne's interest as Lynton had shared what she had learned about him with him. He quizzed Dr. McCormack on Ambrogio, and basically got the same information that Lynton had shared with him. Then, McCormack began to explain vampires as legends related specifically to the Philippines. No doubt he was a pompous ass, but he was a knowledgeable one. He reared backed in his leather chair, propped his feet up on his desk to show off his expensive Italian Bruno Magli shoes which had been made famous in the O.J. Simpson trial. What follows is the discourse minus most of the self-serving, back-patting self aggrandizement that he liberally sprinkled into the oration. This was a man so impressed with himself that he probably had calluses on his hands from patting himself on the back so much.

As he explained to Wayne, he puffed out his chest and acted as if he was a great potentate of knowledge. "An Aswang or Asuwang is a vampire-like mythical creature in Filipino folklore and is the subject of a wide variety of myths and stories. Spanish colonists noted that the Aswang was the most feared among the mythical creatures of the Philippines, even in the 16th century."

"The myth of the Aswang is well known throughout the Philippines, except in the Ilocos region, which is the only region that does not have an equivalent myth. It is especially popular in the Western Visayan regions such as

LYNTON AND THE VAMPIRE
AT TAGAYTAY MANOR NEAR THE VOLCANO
THAT SPEWED SORROW RATHER THAN LAVA

Capiz, Iloilo, Negros, Bohol, Masbate, Aklan, Antique and Siquijor. Other regional names for the Aswang include tik-tik, wak-wak and sok-sok.

"Aswang refers specifically to a ghoulish were-dog, which is where the word comes from - Ang Aso or the dog in English. Aswang is derived from Sanskrit words swan and ang. Shwan means dog and ang means body."

"The creature is a combination of a vampire and a werewolf. Sometimes this creature is called the bal-bal or ghoul. Aswang stories and definitions vary greatly from region to region and person to person, and no particular set of characteristics can be ascribed to the term. The creature is usually depicted as female."

McCormack got up briefly, walked over to the window and looked out at the world famous Wreck Beach below the campus. He got off the subject and said, "Love to look at all the naked bodies lying on the beach out there. The students here have no sense of decorum. What the world needs is more formality, a return to traditional values where modesty prevails."

LYNTON AND THE VAMPIRE
AT TAGAYTAY MANOR NEAR THE VOLCANO
THAT SPEWED SORROW RATHER THAN LAVA

Of course Wayne was thinking that if McCormack believed the world needed a bit more respect for traditional values and decorum, why was he looking at the naked women on the beach below?

McCormack took a deep breath and obviously was enjoying one last look at the naked women below, and then he turned and took his seat again. He continued. "The wide variety of descriptions in the Aswang stories makes it difficult to settle upon a fixed definition of Aswang appearances or activities. However, several common themes that differentiate Aswangs from other mythological creatures do emerge: Aswangs are shape-shifters. Stories recount Aswangs living as regular townspeople. As regular townspeople, they are quiet, shy and elusive. At night, they transform into creatures such as a cat, bat, bird, boar or most often, a dog. They enjoy eating unborn fetuses and small children, favouring livers and hearts. Some have long noses, which they use to suck the children out of their mothers' wombs. Some are so thin that they can hide themselves behind a bamboo post. They are fast and silent. Some also make noises, like the Tik-Tik, the name being derived from the sounds it produces, which are louder the farther away the Aswang is, to confuse its potential victim; and the Bubuu, an aggressive kind of Aswang that makes a sound of a laying hen. An Aswang, unlike a vampire, can go out in the daylight. These creatures are not harmed by sunlight. They are day walkers. Aswangs can also be befriended, they can talk to you like any normal human being: they laugh, cry, get mad, hurt and feel envy. These creatures do not harm their neighbours. Neighbours were said to be exempted from their target victims for food, hence the Filipino saying, *Better an aswang than a thief.* They search for food in far away places that it would not be too obvious for them. Aswangs are said to be vulnerable during daytime because during that time they do not have the excessive inhuman strength that they have in their night-time prowl. Aswangs are physically much more like humans in the daytime; they only change their appearance at night when they feel they are in need of food. It has been said that if an Aswang married a human, upon their wedding, his or her mate can become an Aswang as well but rarely can they reproduce. The couple may hunt together at night but will go in separate directions, either to avoid detection or because they do not like to share their meal. There have been instances where Aswangs have actually wed vampires. Their similarities make them good mates. Sometimes Aswangs also forget they are Aswangs."

Wayne was enthralled with McCormack's discourse, but of course, he did not believe in vampires. Yet, it might be helpful to Lynton, so he listened intently as McCormack continued. "Like vampires, Aswangs are repelled or killed by using garlic, salt, and religious artefacts like holy water, crucifixes and rosaries. They are also killed using a whip made entirely of a stingray's tail, which may also be used to repel the creature as Aswangs are said to be scared of the sound made by the whip slashing through the air. It is also said that they cannot step on holy consecrated ground. Decapitation is also a way to destroy an Aswang. Certain prayers posted on doors may also repel Aswangs, a good example of which is the orange and black bead bracelets worn by newborn Filipino babies. It is said that to spot an Aswang at daytime, look at their eyes. The person in front of you is an Aswang if your reflection is upside-down. A kind of oil made by albularyos is used to detect if an Aswang is near the premises. It is said that the oil will boil if an Aswang is near. So that is pretty much it – no vampires per se in the Philippines, just Aswangs."

LYNTON AND THE VAMPIRE
AT TAGAYTAY MANOR NEAR THE VOLCANO
THAT SPEWED SORROW RATHER THAN LAVA

It was disconcerting to Wayne to realize that such a pompous, arrogant jerk was so brilliant. If only he had a bit of humility, he might actually be a pretty decent guy.

Wayne, still wanting more information, said, "So, according to legend there are no vampires in the Philippines, only Aswangs?"

"Ah, I did not say categorically that there were no vampires there. You see, there was, as you know, according to legend, a vampire named Ambrogio, and he is rumoured to have left his native Italy for the Transylvanian Mountains in Romania. We all know from Bram Stoker's book *Dracula*, which is based somewhat on the real life Vlad the Impaler, that Transylvania is famous for at least one vampire. However, Ambrogio, it is rumoured, was actually welcomed there by Vlad the Impaler, or as Stoker called him Count Dracula. Now Vlad had a loyal assistant who came from the Philippines, as we all know the Filipino reputation for being loyal servants even to this day. This assistant was rumoured to be an Aswang. His name was Quinton, according to some accounts. Vlad assigned this loyal servant to the estate of his friend Ambrogio."

LYNTON AND THE VAMPIRE
AT TAGAYTAY MANOR NEAR THE VOLCANO
THAT SPEWED SORROW RATHER THAN LAVA

Wayne could not believe it when he heard the name Quinton as Lynton had shared the name of Lekman's servant with him. Things were beginning to connect up, but they were almost too fantastic to believe. He said, as Dr. McCormack scratched his forehead, "So, whatever happened to Ambrogio? Any rumours at all. I mean he would be a couple thousand years old today, at least. Still, legends are fun to hear. What do you think?"

"I think you are a cynical man. You only believe what you can see and hear. Billions believe in the Bible, the Qur'an, the Vedas, the Dhammapada, the Torah, the Dao de jing, the Guru Granth Sahib and the Book of Morman. OK, they may contain mistruths and are, in many cases, just retelling of ancient stories. Yet, I believe there is some truth in them, some basis for fact. For that reason, I put some credence in the stories of Ambrogio and his loyal servant. Could a man live for 2000 years? No, I don't believe that. Still, as a scholar, you know that we cannot explain all things. We know one plus one equals two, but why is that always true. Is there ever a time when one plus one might equal three? I am relatively sure the answer is no – never, but I am not 100% certain."

LYNTON AND THE VAMPIRE
AT TAGAYTAY MANOR NEAR THE VOLCANO
THAT SPEWED SORROW RATHER THAN LAVA

Wayne, his respect for McCormack's intelligence growing, said, "So, any idea about what happened to Ambrogio? Obviously, he was not a real vampire and is dead now, but what of his descendants?"

McCormick let a smile slowly creep across his lips. "Well, Ambrogio took another name, a name that he apparently frequently used the rest of his life, wherever he spent it. He left Transylvania in 1466 when Vlad was imprisoned for 10 years in Hungary, as he fell out of favour and feared retribution."

"He took a Spanish name and travelled under it for many years until he simply disappears in 1472. No one knows where he was, but during the communist rule of Romania a man claiming to be Ambrogio was an advisor to the head of the Communist Party, Nicolae Ceausescu. It was claimed by many that Ambrogio had returned. In fact, this person claiming to be Ambrogio even lived in the same castle that Ambrogio had lived in hundreds of years before. Apparently with the blessing of the Romanian government of Nicolae Ceausescu this man is rumoured to have wielded tremendous power. Ceauşescu's rise to power was often credited to Ambrogio's mystical power that was used to Nicolae Ceausescu's advantage."

Wayne was now sitting on the edge of his seat as the story became more intriguing. McCormack continued. "As most intelligent people know, that Hollywood buffoon, Ronald Reagan, was obsessed with destroying communism, and his wife Nancy regularly consulted psychics." He looked Wayne directly in the eyes as he chuckled, "Of course, she should have been consulting a good neurologist to deal with Reagan's deteriorating mental state."

They both laughed and then McCormack went on with his story. "Anyway, one of her psychics told her that Nicolae Ceausescu's wife was friends with a man named Ambrogio who was a great seer and, if offered sanctuary in the USA, he would, no doubt, use his power to help Reagan. There was an attempt to get him to the USA, but the Ceausescu's would not let him leave, as they felt their hold on power was becoming tenuous, and they needed him. They were right, they did need him, as the wild spending to secure the world for corporations by Reagan finally paid off in 1989 when Ceausescu was killed."

LYNTON AND THE VAMPIRE
AT TAGAYTAY MANOR NEAR THE VOLCANO
THAT SPEWED SORROW RATHER THAN LAVA

Wayne, an astute scholar on communism and how it was used as justification by the USA for all kinds of nefarious deeds, including the suppression of its own citizens, was enthralled by how the orchestrated fall of communism and the securing of the world for corporate domination actually involved Ambrogio. He asked McCormack what happened to this man named Ambrogio after the fall of Ceausescu.

Wiping his brow, McCormack said, "Well, no one knows for sure. Apparently with Reagan mercifully out of the White House in 1989, there was no longer any interest in him coming to the USA, as it would have created a scandal bringing in an ex- communist adviser to Ceausescu as an adviser to the now even more mentally deteriorating former President. A few years later, Ambrogio took up the same Spanish name his predecessor used and left for – are you ready now Wayne?"

Wayne nodded his head yes, as McCormack said, "The Philippines with his servant Quinton Sagrando. Ambrogio travelled under the Spanish name Lekman Lopez."

LYNTON AND THE VAMPIRE
AT TAGAYTAY MANOR NEAR THE VOLCANO
THAT SPEWED SORROW RATHER THAN LAVA

CHAPTER 7

WHERE EVIL ABIDES AS WINGS OF DEATH

FLUTTER IN THE CLOUDS OF DARKNESS

Faith offers the invisible shelter of an angel's wing.
This sunlight-loving Lynton and friends,
Saw evil and wanted to confront it
As hope and justice the loving Lynton lends.

Ah, but he who stalks by night
Exhales from all he eats and drinks, and embraces
The ever sweet ambrosia and the nectar red
As he is the evil undead.

He trifles with the winds and with the clouds that glide,
About the way unto the Cross, he laughs as he sings.
The spirit is an evil pilgrimage; that dark guide.
While others weep, he laughs as evil springs.

All those that he should cherish shrink from him with fear,
And some that waxen bold by his tranquility,
Endeavour hard some grievance from his heart to tear,
And make on him the trial of their ferocity.

LYNTON AND THE VAMPIRE
AT TAGAYTAY MANOR NEAR THE VOLCANO
THAT SPEWED SORROW RATHER THAN LAVA

Within the bread and wine outspread for his repast
To mingle dust and dirty evil they essay,
And everything he touches, forth is slyly cast,
Others scourge themselves, if e'er their feet trod his way.

Word was spreading through Tagaytay that the volcanologists were concerned about Taal, as it was rumbling to life, but there seemed to be no build up of lava. Rather, it appeared that it was just venting steam. Or as one observer offered, "it was simply spewing sorrow rather than lava, because of the recent tragic death of Diana Rodriguez."

On the speaker phone, Wayne shared all he had learned with the girls, and as he prepared to hang up, an ill-feeling seemed to overwhelm him as he pled with Lynton. "Be careful darling. I am taking the next plane there. I don't believe in vampires, but I believe in evil, and this Lekman Lopez, and maybe the Perrdonez family is evil. I feel it in my bones. I am scared for you as I have never been before. Not the voice of doom which you fought, not the vanity which you defeated, nor charlatan in Taal had me this scared. I leave tomorrow and will arrive there in 2 days."

LYNTON AND THE VAMPIRE
AT TAGAYTAY MANOR NEAR THE VOLCANO
THAT SPEWED SORROW RATHER THAN LAVA

Lynton, never one prone to fear, said, "Darling, I appreciate your love and concern, but I will be OK. You have work to do there. Do it, and come when it is finished."

Wayne, without hesitation, said, "No, my work is you and your safety. I am coming."

Lynton, smiling because she knew she had someone who genuinely loved her as no one had ever loved her before, said, "OK, boss!"

Wayne, accustomed to her saying that on occasion, still could not fight back laughter as he said, "Yeah, right."

Channa, after Lynton hung up, said, "OK, we have battled demons, vain people and charlatans. How do we battle a vampire?"

Lynton pulled out a book she had gotten from the library and said, "We go into battle with weapons drawn."

Ingrid, perhaps the most religious of the three said, "I say the cross is the most effective weapon."

LYNTON AND THE VAMPIRE
AT TAGAYTAY MANOR NEAR THE VOLCANO
THAT SPEWED SORROW RATHER THAN LAVA

Lynton, ever practical, said, "The cross keeps the vampire at bay. It does not defeat him. Everyone knows Hollywood's take on the vampire myth. Confront him with a crucifix or garlic to ward him or her off, not kill them. Immersion in running water, cut off the head, stake him in the heart, all these Hollywood techniques derive from real myth, but not all of these myths actually work in the world of darkness we are about to face, or at least there's only a kernel of truth to some of them. There are, according to this book, assuming the vampire hasn't taken precautions against one or all of them, and that he doesn't wake up right before the job is completed, only a few sure-fire methods to defeat the children of the night."

"A vampire's daylight slumber makes him most vulnerable. If would-be killers can find his haven, he's in jeopardy. Most vampires set up defences, however. Here in the Philippines, according to what Wayne related from Professor McCormack, an Aswang may stand watch over Lekman Lopez as he sleeps in his coffin. And then there's the threat of the vampire rising during the day, shielded in the dark recesses of his hiding place, killing whoever dares to threaten him there in the darkness."

LYNTON AND THE VAMPIRE
AT TAGAYTAY MANOR NEAR THE VOLCANO
THAT SPEWED SORROW RATHER THAN LAVA

Suddenly Lynton started laughing and so did Channa and Ingrid. Lynton was almost hysterical with frivolity as she said, "Listen to us. We are intelligent girls. What is wrong with us? We know there are no such things as vampires or Aswangs."

Ingrid, her laughter slowly fading, said, "Are we prepared to kill a human being? We are playing with fire here. Obviously, these idiots may think they are vampires and Aswangs, but we cannot play games with people's lives like this, even if one of them is a murderer and the others may be implicated in the cover up. Shouldn't we go to the police?"

Lynton calmly offered some sage advice. "Hey, there is something very nefarious going on here, but the police are useless. They have proven their incompetence already, and I am still worried about Lupe. So, let's assume Lekman, Quinton," and then she looked over at Ingrid as she continued, "maybe even the Perrdonez family somehow believe this vampire legend or at least are somehow wound up in the whole myth of the thing. Perhaps they are nothing more than an evil cult. The book offers some guidance in how to destroy a vampire. Maybe we could use this knowledge to scare them."

Channa, with preciseness as always, said, "Sure, so what is the method, according to the book, that we use to kill vampires? We let them know we are familiar with it, right? Then they are forewarned that we might be just crazy enough to believe in vampires."

Lynton offered details. "According to the book, in the world of darkness, staking a vampire in the heart only paralyzes him. It doesn't destroy him once and for all. If someone pulls the stake out or it rots away, he rises again and no doubt remembers who assaulted him and seeks revenge on that person or that person's descendants. Assuming no other means of destruction is available; a staked vampire can be immersed in concrete or bricked up behind a wall. That way, they are permanently encased."

"So, we must convince these people that we are serious vampire slayers. A vampire is immune to the effects of poison, but the mortals who serve him are not. Undermine his support system. Drive off or kill his agents and servants and his means of survival is taken away. Sure, he's tipped off that someone is after him, but without backup, his weapons are diminished."

Channa, coldly said, "So, we convince these people we mean business, and that we are willing to kill if necessary. That we really believe in this ridiculousness."

"Yes," offered Lynton. "We convince them that we know the one fool-proof method for death of a vampire. Sunlight is not so easily portable, but it is the only certain method according to the book. At best, a vampire can hide from it, and if he's forced to hide from it without a pre-planned escape route or back door he is going to dissipate, simply turn into dust. This Lekman genuinely believes he is a vampire, so he is probably terrified of sunlight and can fly into panicked frenzies when exposed to it. All of these people are only on the edge of sanity. I know Ingrid that you think Harold is OK, and I hope you are right, but your last love affair proved that sometimes what you see on the surface is an illusion. I love you, but I do not want to see you deceived again. I hope you can understand that, and not have anger toward me."

LYNTON AND THE VAMPIRE
AT TAGAYTAY MANOR NEAR THE VOLCANO
THAT SPEWED SORROW RATHER THAN LAVA

Ingrid replied, "I could not have anger with someone who loves me so dearly. I know you want what is best for me. I shall not falter if Harold is somehow involved, but I believe he is in the dark almost as much as we are. Tomorrow night is his 30th birthday, and he says that his family is insisting he go to Lekman's for a special party. I am concerned about his safety."

"We shall be party crashers then. We will make an appearance at the party and confront this evil once and for all. First Ingrid, contact Harold, as we need to talk to him. We need to take him into our confidence and see if he is really with us or against us. We must also see Lupe, as I think she is vulnerable to the machinations of Lekman Lopez and she may have something to do with tomorrow night's rendezvous at Tagaytay Manor. She has been marked for death I believe. These people are dangerous, very dangerous."

I am now going to tell you something so strange that it will require all your faith in my veracity to believe my story. It was a mild summer evening, and Lynton and her two friends decided they needed to get Lupe to somewhere

LYNTON AND THE VAMPIRE
AT TAGAYTAY MANOR NEAR THE VOLCANO
THAT SPEWED SORROW RATHER THAN LAVA

safe outside Tagaytay. The girls rode in Channa's car through the beautiful forest vista that led to Lupe's home. The sun was setting with all its melancholy splendour behind the golden horizon, and the stream that flowed beside the road, and passes under the steep old bridge seemed particularly peaceful, reflecting the image of the red car as it sped along the highway under the capable tutelage of Channa, whose driving was as precise as her diction.

All this seemingly peaceful tranquility began to fade gradually as a dark cloud appeared on the distant horizon just as they pulled up in front of the hillside, parked and headed down toward Lupe's home. Looking around them in the fading twilight, Lynton felt that they were all cursed. She looked back over her shoulder at Tagaytay Manor as the sun made its final dip into the oblivion of night. Suddenly she said, "I curse my conceited incredulity, my despicable affectation of superiority, my blindness, my obstinacy—all now that it is too late. I was distracted."

Ingrid and Channa stood startled and shouted "What are you talking about?"

LYNTON AND THE VAMPIRE
AT TAGAYTAY MANOR NEAR THE VOLCANO
THAT SPEWED SORROW RATHER THAN LAVA

Lynton, a look of determination on her face, said, "Come on. We have so little time. I know why everything hinges on Harold's 30th birthday. Come, Lupe is in serious danger."

A thin film of mist was stealing like smoke, marking the distance to Lupe's house in a transparent veil; and the darkness was getting more intense as Ingrid and Channa gave each other a puzzled look, but they knew Lynton's stubbornness of thought. She would tell them what she knew when she was ready and not before. There were no stars out, but the moonlight was dancing about in the darkness as if singing a melancholy song of discontent. The effect of the dancing moon in such a state was manifold. It acted on dreams, it acted on lunacy, it acted on nervous people, and it had a harrowing influence on the coming evil. The moon, the night was full of foreboding and magnetic influence. There was no gaiety coming from inside Lupe's house, as Lynton could see in front of her how all its windows flashed and twinkled with a false splendour, as if unseen hands had lit up the rooms in a sense of despair. There was something unseen and unexplained, something evil going on inside.

LYNTON AND THE VAMPIRE
AT TAGAYTAY MANOR NEAR THE VOLCANO
THAT SPEWED SORROW RATHER THAN LAVA

Looking back up the hillside, Lynton saw the lights come on in Tagaytay Manor and she looked upward and noticed a large bat flying overhead, wings flapping incessantly as its giant outline passed in front of the moon, just as had occurred the night they rescued Ingrid from Lekman Lopez. He had, through hypnosis, she thought, made them think he was a bat. The girls looked upward as the flapping of the wings could be heard as the bat disappeared into the darkness. They listened intently as the flapping slowly faded away down the hillside that led to the boat ramp where the boats plied the waters to the volcano.

As the girls approached Lupe's door, from inside emerged none other than Patrice Perrdonez who had a hideous sort of coloured turban on her head, and who was gazing all the time right into the girl's eyes, nodding and grinning derisively towards them with gleaming eyes and large white eye-balls, and her teeth set as if in fury portending mayhem. Smiling broadly she simply said, as she headed up the hillside, "good evening ladies."

Head bowed, Lupe, with tears rolling down her cheeks, said, "Come in. Despair rules our home."

LYNTON AND THE VAMPIRE
AT TAGAYTAY MANOR NEAR THE VOLCANO
THAT SPEWED SORROW RATHER THAN LAVA

There was a sombreness as Richie sat, not smoking a cigarette as usual, but with his head buried in his hands. Meanwhile, Lupe, though anxious, appeared relatively calm. There was a certain resignation in her face, almost as if she was ready to accept fate.

There were candles on the kitchen table. Lupe eased into a chair sitting up straight as if she were tied to the back of it; her slender figure enveloped in the soft silk dress she was wearing, embroidered with flowers, and lined with thick brocade. Sitting beside her was Harold Perrdonez, who was glum. The whole scene was surreal, but Lynton understood it instantly. "They have one of your children don't they, and they have threatened the child if you do not show up for Harold's party tonight. Furthermore, they have told you bringing in the police will only lead to your child's harm. You, Harold, were hiding in the back room while Patrice was here, as you came to try and warn Lupe and Richie to get away as quickly as possible. Only you were too late."

Harold was vehemently nodding affirmatively, while saying "yes."

LYNTON AND THE VAMPIRE
AT TAGAYTAY MANOR NEAR THE VOLCANO
THAT SPEWED SORROW RATHER THAN LAVA

Ingrid and Channa were mesmerized by what Lynton knew. She continued. "Harold, you know now that the face you saw that night when you were a child was Patrice. It was she who was in your room. It was she who killed your mother so that she could become mistress of the house and marry your father. My guess is that your father was unaware of the plot at first, Patrice being sent there by Lekman Lopez, along with his trusted aid Quinton Sagrando. However, your father is now under their spell, controlled by the evil that emanates from Lekman Lopez."

All Harold could do was nod his head up and down. Meanwhile, Channa and Ingrid were simply blown away by what Lynton had deduced. Lynton walked over and sat beside a despondent Richie and placed her hand on his left leg, looked over at Lupe and said. "Don't worry, we are going to work our way though this. We will not allow evil to triumph. They are going to perform a ceremony tonight Harold. I perceived something of languor and exhaustion stealing over me earlier today, as I was sensing an impending crisis. Believe me, we three girls have been in tougher situations than this and so far, we have always come out on top. We are tough and resilient."

LYNTON AND THE VAMPIRE
AT TAGAYTAY MANOR NEAR THE VOLCANO
THAT SPEWED SORROW RATHER THAN LAVA

Lynton was a small woman. She was slender, and wonderfully graceful. Her complexion was rich and brilliant; her features were small and beautifully formed; her eyes large, dark, and lustrous; her hair was quite wonderful, so magnificently thick and long when it was down about her shoulders. It was exquisitely fine and soft, and in colour a rich very deep dark brown, almost, but not quiet black. She was not only beautiful but imposing both physically, even though short, she had broad, strong shoulders as manifested in someone who was a volleyball player and her legs both at the thighs and in the calves were muscular, not in a masculine way, but in a way that made her muscular tone feminine and even erotic. Intellectually, she was a quick study who was slow and methodical in her analysis of any situation. She exuded confidence both physically and mentally. This was one of those times when these traits helped put those there with her at ease, and made them confident in her ability to ascertain the situation and foster a solution.

They all looked to her for guidance, as she worked diligently in her mind to come up with a solution. One could almost see the wheels turning in her head.

LYNTON AND THE VAMPIRE
AT TAGAYTAY MANOR NEAR THE VOLCANO
THAT SPEWED SORROW RATHER THAN LAVA

Channa broke the silence. "What do we do Lynton?"

"First and foremost," said a determined Lynton, "we make sure we do as we are told, within reason that is, so that no harm will come to Lupe's and Richie's daughter. Patrice, Paul, Quinton and Lekman have no fear of us now. They do not care what we three know, because they have Lupe's child as insurance." She then turned to Harold. "You know what they have planned for you?"

Harold, very timidly replied, "I'm not sure."

Lynton did not hesitate in her reply. "You can be sure Harold that I know. You are a chosen one – the Incomby is what you are called in the book I read. When you were a child, you were singled out to offer your body to Lekman Lopez. I know it sounds fantastic, but these people actually believe that Lekman is the vampire Ambrogio. According to legend, he needs a new body periodically to replenish himself and continue his blood lust. It must be done on the Incomby's 30th birthday at exactly the time he was born. You, Harold, are the chosen one who will reinvigorate him, make him young again."

LYNTON AND THE VAMPIRE
AT TAGAYTAY MANOR NEAR THE VOLCANO
THAT SPEWED SORROW RATHER THAN LAVA

Ingrid, never one to mince words, said "Damn girl. You are good, but what do we do?"

Lynton looked at Lupe, "Well, I know Lupe is willing to do whatever it takes to get her child free of their clutches. You see, they need the mother of 6 according to the ritual, only the mother of 6 has the mystical powers they need. My guess is that Lupe is also the sixth child of her mother Anna. Am I right Lupe?"

Lupe nodded her head affirmatively. Then Lynton continued. "And you were born in June – right?"

Almost in a whisper, barely audible, Lupe said, "yes."

Lynton said, "There you have it. The sixth child, born on the sixth month with six children of her own – 6 – 6 – 6, the sign of the beast!"

Instant recognition of the significance was plastered on everyone's face. Real or not, these people were evil, and everything they were doing was grounded in what they perceived as reality, according to ancient ritual.

LYNTON AND THE VAMPIRE
AT TAGAYTAY MANOR NEAR THE VOLCANO
THAT SPEWED SORROW RATHER THAN LAVA

Lynton, though not particularly religious, like her boyfriend Wayne, was somewhat of a Bible scholar, having often studied it out of curiosity about how it had been used for both good and bad throughout history. She shared a bit of knowledge with those there in Lupe's home. "Here is wisdom says Revelations. Let him that hath understanding count the number of a man and his number is six hundred and sixty-six."

"This number has great significance for those who fear the number and those who revere the number. For many superstitious people, just saying the number causes palpitations of the heart as it conjures up horrible images of deviltry, the black arts, occult manifestations and the final days of Biblical prophecy. To those who worship at the devil's altar, it is a glorious number, symbolizing the anti-Christ whom they honour above all others."

Those gathered there hung on every word as Lynton's oratorical skills rivalled that of a hellfire and damnation preacher on the stump rousing souls to come to Christ and turn their backs on the devil. She was a woman on fire with passion and commitment.

LYNTON AND THE VAMPIRE
AT TAGAYTAY MANOR NEAR THE VOLCANO
THAT SPEWED SORROW RATHER THAN LAVA

She walked over to the kitchen table, picked up a glass of water and took a sip, then continued her oration. "Revelation Chapter 13, verse 1 says, 'Then I stood on the sand of the sea and I saw a beast rising up out of the sea.' Verse 11 goes on, 'then I saw another beast coming out of the earth, and he had two horns like a lamb and spoke like a dragon.' I know, it is a bit ridiculous, a talking dragon, but to understand what is going on we have to suspend ourselves from common sense and reality. So, there are two beasts that bear the mark 666 mentioned in Revelations and these beasts are being called upon by Lekman, Patrice, Paul and Quinton tomorrow night to bring new life to Lekman, who is under the delusion that he is a vampire."

Lupe, a peculiar look on her face, said, "But I believe in the devil. I believe in what it says in Revelations. I believe that the mark of the beast is 666."

Lynton, deadly serious, replied, "Yes, and that is important. They must have a person who believes in the power of 666, and they intend to sacrifice the soul of Harold and your body Lupe to the beast or beasts they hope to conjure up."

LYNTON AND THE VAMPIRE
AT TAGAYTAY MANOR NEAR THE VOLCANO
THAT SPEWED SORROW RATHER THAN LAVA

Looks of intense fear descended like an ancient plague upon the faces of all present, except, for some reason, Lupe. Channa, measured with serious intent, said "What, you are telling me that these lunatics are going to offer a human sacrifice so Lekman can be awarded as a prize the soul of Harold while Lupe lies gutted on an altar?"

Lynton, calm and collected, replied "Yes, that is what I am telling you. Wayne and I have discussed this in detail. The expert on vampires he saw at the University of British Columbia shared a book with him that details all the incantations and spells that must be cast in order for a vampire to continue with his immortality. It is not the stuff of Hollywood. It is the stuff that has been practiced by deranged minds throughout history. None of we here, well, at least most of us, believe in vampires, but I think we can all believe in man's cruelty, and man's oft times insane beliefs in the mystical. These four people are all deranged, and they are willing to commit heinous acts in support of what they believe. Harold, your real mother was murdered because of these beliefs. You were nearly molested as a child, because it is written that on the child's third birthday, the child should be defiled as part of a ritual dictated by the ancient text that details the procedures for preparing the Incomby for the sacrifice of his soul. The Incomby will not be killed, but he might as well be, as he will be rendered insane by the acts perpetrated upon him."

"Historically speaking, in documented cases where this ritual has been performed, the Incomby have seemingly always wound up in mental institutions. There is no known explanation for this, other than perhaps that the strain of what these people experienced created such shock that they were unable to psychologically deal with it, thus their minds snapped. There were three certified cases, and in all instances, the perpetrators escaped. One case was in Romania at the time of Vlad, and with all Vlad's misdeeds, a case of one human sacrifice and one man going insane would hardly be cause for concern. Another case occurred in Ambrogio's native Italy, and, again the perpetrators were never apprehended. The third case mentioned in the book was in Spain, and strangely enough, a man named Quinton Sagrando was actually questioned by authorities as his master, who mysteriously disappeared after the murder, was a prime suspect. Lack of evidence led to the case being dropped and Sagrando left Spain almost immediately."

LYNTON AND THE VAMPIRE AT TAGAYTAY MANOR NEAR THE VOLCANO THAT SPEWED SORROW RATHER THAN LAVA

Ingrid, boiling with rage, barked "So what the hell are we to do?"

Channa, calm and collected, interjected, "What we have done before. Kick some demon butt."

Lynton, as always, proud to have her loyal friends by her side, said, "Hey, I am not sure I believe in demons in a physical sense, despite what we have all experienced in the past, but these insane psychopaths do believe in them. Me, I believe in our friendship, our devotion to one another and our dedication to justice and fair play. Demon or no demon, we are going to kick some serious butt. Patrice, Paul, Quinton and Lekman are the forces of darkness, but they are about to go into battle against the forces of light."

Richie, who had been silent through the whole ordeal, and managed to not pick up a cigarette, said "I have been a fool for so long, not realizing what I had in a loyal wife and loving children. I am at your service, ready to do anything necessary to protect my wife and children."

Lynton replied, "Your devotion will be tested, then."

LYNTON AND THE VAMPIRE
AT TAGAYTAY MANOR NEAR THE VOLCANO
THAT SPEWED SORROW RATHER THAN LAVA

Smiling with determination, Richie replied "Test away little girl. Test away."

"Sometimes," replied Lynton, "doing nothing takes as much courage as forging into battle. All of you must be patient. We have the rest of today, tonight and tomorrow during the day to prepare for battle. I know my dear Wayne will understand that I must use my feminine wiles on Quinton Sagrando to gain access to Tagaytay Manor. I do not see myself as such, but there are those who claim my body is beauteous to behold. Why not perform in the office of these demons of gloom? And take myself before Quinton decked in alluring dress, sprinkled delicately with incense, perfumed myrrh, and with genuflexions ingratiate myself to him. I shall play with his emotions, but my aim is to ultimately cunningly conspire to steal his feeble heart and like a youngling bird that trembles in its nest, I'll pluck his heart right out; within its own blood drowned, and just like what he desires, I will finally to satiate my beastliness, throw it with intense disdain upon the ground, step on it, crush it with passion for righteousness and the dignity that they wish to steal from these good people here before us now. I will get they key to that which is hidden."

LYNTON AND THE VAMPIRE
AT TAGAYTAY MANOR NEAR THE VOLCANO
THAT SPEWED SORROW RATHER THAN LAVA

Upon finishing her soliloquy, Lynton burst out with laughter, and those there joined her, as they all realized she was just trying to lighten everyone up from the sombre mood they were all in. The laughter lightened everyone's mood, but Lynton, deadly serious, continued. "Now, I will go to visit Quinton Sagrando, but I shall not tear out his heart, but only tear into the evil that controls it."

Lynton looked over at Ingrid, and with a coy smile, as she pointed to Harold, said "You girl are to make this man forget his troubles for awhile," and then she winked at her, "as only a woman of your seductive nature can. You two spend the day as light-hearted as possible, because the battle that lies ahead will not be easy."

She walked over to Lupe, took her by the hand and led her over to the sofa where Richie sat. She lightly pushed her down beside him and, knowing Richie needed encouragement and a pat on the back as he struggled to change his nature, said "You and this good man comfort each other with your love," as she reached down and picked up his pack of cigarettes which had been unopened, continuing with her praise. "I'll take these and gladly give them a toss down the hillside, because you have conquered your addiction to one of society's most wretched habits that enriches those who profit off human misery. You are now ready to smoke from the pyre of love rather than the pyre of human weakness to corporate manipulation."

Through all this, Lupe was stoically quiet, almost as if she had knowledge the others did not. Lynton sensed she was hiding something, but did not press the matter, as she assumed it was either unimportant or that she would reveal it at the proper time. Yet, it did cause her concern.

She then turned to Channa and said, "Come on girl, help me put my war paint on, because I am going into battle where evil abides as wings of death flutter in the clouds of darkness."

LYNTON AND THE VAMPIRE
AT TAGAYTAY MANOR NEAR THE VOLCANO
THAT SPEWED SORROW RATHER THAN LAVA

CHAPTER 8

VULNERABLE TO A KICK IN THE GROIN

Lynton can see that which is hidden from others.
Towards the Heavens she sees the sacred grail.
She calmly stretches forth her pious arms,
Whereon lightening from the lucid spirit veil
Strikes that incessant evil that swarms.

Oh blest be thou, she who fights pain,
Like some divine redress for our infirmities,
And like the most refreshing and the purest rain,
To sanctify the good for saintly ecstasies.

For her, heaven will grant a favoured chair,
Among the Sainted Legion and the blissful ones,
That of the endless feast she will accord a share
For her virtues, kindness and offering love's thrones.

She knows that sorrow is not nobleness alone,
Which never may corrupted be by hell nor curse.
She knows, in order to enwreathe the mystic crown
She must inspire the ages and the universe.

LYNTON AND THE VAMPIRE
AT TAGAYTAY MANOR NEAR THE VOLCANO
THAT SPEWED SORROW RATHER THAN LAVA

The fabled buried jewels of pirates old,
The undiscovered resources beneath the sea,
Of gems, that unto her could never behold,
Beside her never shine more brilliant than she.

For it shall be engendered from the purest fire
Of rays primeval, from the holy hearth amassed,
Of which the eyes of mortals, in their sheen entire,
Before her are tarnished mirrors, sad and overcast.

As Wayne made his way on the ferry to the airport in downtown Vancouver from Vancouver Island where he lived, he was doing research on vampires, frantically going from one web site to another trying to find something that might help Lynton. Now Wayne was a notorious spendthrift, and probably one of the few people left in the civilized world who did not own a cell-phone. He relied on a computer and communicated primarily through Skype, Facebook and Yahoo Messenger, because he felt that paying for the internet was in itself a travesty, as he sincerely believed that all people should have access to the internet regardless of their economic status. Like healthcare, food and shelter, to him it was a human right.

LYNTON AND THE VAMPIRE
AT TAGAYTAY MANOR NEAR THE VOLCANO
THAT SPEWED SORROW RATHER THAN LAVA

With this in mind, it should be understood that he was unable to contact Lynton since he had no cell-phone for a direct call. Anyway, she was notorious for turning off her phone. Yet, Wayne desperately wanted to discuss what he had just discovered through painstaking research. He dashed off an e-mail, beseeching her to contact him as soon as possible.

You see, Wayne had just discovered something that was going to be crucial to Lynton understanding exactly what was going to happen the night of the transformation of Lekman Lopez through his Incomby. Try to imagine reddish green, not the dull brown you get when you mix the two pigments together, but rather a color that is somewhat like red and somewhat like green. Or, instead, try to picture yellowish blue, not green, but a hue similar to both yellow and blue. Is your mind drawing a blank? That's because, even though those colors exist, you have probably never seen them. Red-green and yellow-blue are the so-called "forbidden colors." Composed of pairs of hues whose light frequencies automatically cancel each other out in the human eye, they're supposed to be impossible to see simultaneously. This limitation results from the way we perceive colour in the first place. Cells in the retina called "opponent neurons" fire when stimulated by incoming red light, and this flurry of activity tells the brain we're looking at something red. Those same opponent neurons are inhibited by green light, and the absence of activity tells the brain we're seeing green. Similarly, yellow light excites another set of opponent neurons, but blue light damps them. While most colors induce a mixture of effects in both sets of neurons, which our brains can decode to identify the component parts, red light exactly cancels the effect of green light (and yellow exactly cancels blue), so we can never perceive those colors coming from the same place.

Wayne's discovery of information that was readily available, but was privy to only those curious enough to look, was not in and of itself important until you reflected back upon something that happened long ago. As he continued to read about vampires, Aswangs and other manifestations of evil, he paid no notice to a picture on one page of a woman who had been rumoured to be an Aswang. He would not have been able to understand the connection anyway, the painting done in 1845 was absolutely, without any doubt, the image of Patrice Perrdonez.

LYNTON AND THE VAMPIRE
AT TAGAYTAY MANOR NEAR THE VOLCANO
THAT SPEWED SORROW RATHER THAN LAVA

Now, Wayne had never seen her, so he had no reason to assume that the woman was one and the same with the woman who had only a few hours before smiled at Lynton as she walked out of Lupe's home. However, what was even more interesting was what he read below the photo: *It is widely believed that the demons summoned from hell in the ceremony of the Incomby are not visible to the normal person, as these demons induce a mixture of effects in which normal brains cannot decode to identify the component parts, red light exactly cancels the effect of green light (and yellow exactly cancels blue), so individuals can never perceive those colors coming from the same place; consequently, the image is not seen by those who are not Aswangs or vampires. This does not mean the demons are not there, only that they are not perceivable to the normal person's eye. Thus, when reports are filed by normal people about what was seen in these ceremonies, tales of people interacting with entities that were not there are common.*

As Wayne boarded the plane for Shanghai, where he would have an 8 hour layover before continuing to Manila, Lynton was getting ready to "vamp" Quinton Sagrando.

LYNTON AND THE VAMPIRE
AT TAGAYTAY MANOR NEAR THE VOLCANO
THAT SPEWED SORROW RATHER THAN LAVA

Lynton had learned the term *vamp* from Wayne while they were conversing on Skype. It seems that she was actually vamping him without realizing it. Wayne, who enjoyed her coy little games of internet seduction, through years of experience with women, was not easy prey for vamping, but with Lynton, he enjoyed the chase. She made him feel like a teenager again. Having learned the term from Wayne, Lynton now used it when talking to Channa about what she was up to with Quinton. "I am going to do what Wayne calls vamping. In other words, I am going to use my femininity to get Quinton Sagrando to let me into Tagaytay Manor so that I might as it were, get a lay of the land so that we might be better prepared for what will ensue tomorrow night when Lupe and Harold go to the mansion."

Channa, not particularly religious, nonetheless was gravely concerned about Lynton. She walked over to her suitcase, opened it and came out with a crucifix at the end of a necklace. "Here, I know you aren't religious, but I would feel better if you took this. I know it does not kill a vampire, but I know it can ward them off. Hey, even if he isn't a vampire, he thinks he is one, so maybe it will work."

LYNTON AND THE VAMPIRE
AT TAGAYTAY MANOR NEAR THE VOLCANO
THAT SPEWED SORROW RATHER THAN LAVA

Lynton, smiling as she fondled the necklace, replied, "Unfortunately my dear Channa, this is a cheap necklace. It must be 100% pure silver to work – kind of like a werewolf requiring a 100% silver bullet."

Channa got a stern look on her face, and said "OK smarty. I don't need your frivolity here. This is serious business, and if this fellow just thinks he is a vampire but is not, he won't be aware this isn't real silver. Take it."

Not wanting to disturb her further, Lynton took it and said, "Thanks for your concern dear friend. It means a lot to me."

"So, you taking my car I suppose?"

Lynton, with the usual shrug of her shoulders, and the quizzical look that was so endearing, replied, "Well, if it is available?"

"Of course it is available. It always is. One of these days you need to get that cheap boyfriend of yours to buy you a car."

LYNTON AND THE VAMPIRE
AT TAGAYTAY MANOR NEAR THE VOLCANO
THAT SPEWED SORROW RATHER THAN LAVA

Laughing, Lynton said, "Hey, he hasn't had a television for over five years, says it is stupid to waste money on 350 channels, when they are all junk. He has never had a cell phone. He has never paid over 500 pesos (about $12.50 Canadian dollars) for a pair of shoes. He takes in his own drink crystals to restaurants, because he says sodas cost too much. He walks 3 kilometres to meet me at work because he doesn't want to spend the 11 pesos (about 30 cents) to take the Jeepney, and you think this guy is going to sprang for a car?"

Channa, shaking her head, said "He is the one you need to vamp. That guy is the cheapest man alive, and the irony is that he could afford all those things."

"According to him, and I quote, "You and my children will benefit from my frugality some day, so stop complaining."

Laughing together, Channa whispered as she hugged her, "I will be by my phone. Girl, don't hesitate to call. Maybe I should go with you. What do you think maybe two girls can vamp him better than one?"

LYNTON AND THE VAMPIRE
AT TAGAYTAY MANOR NEAR THE VOLCANO
THAT SPEWED SORROW RATHER THAN LAVA

"I think he will be more susceptible to one than two. It will make him think I am genuinely interested in him. I should do this alone."

"OK, but I am breaking down the door and going in if you are not back by 6:00PM. I don't want you there when it is dark. You got it?

As she left, Lynton was emphatic as she said, "Got it!"

Quinton Sagrando was absolutely no fool, but whether he was a few hundred years old or a teenager, he was a man, and men are creatures who rarely think with their brain when it comes to women. When woman are around their thought processes originate in an area a bit lower down.

The door had no bell, only a huge old knocker that was so heavy that Lynton had to strain in order to pound it three times in succession. It reverberated throughout the foyer and as the heavy wooden door slowly opened it reminded her of a stone door opening into a crypt. Was she walking into her own tomb? Was this a wise move on her part? She took a deep breath and got her vamping face on.

LYNTON AND THE VAMPIRE
AT TAGAYTAY MANOR NEAR THE VOLCANO
THAT SPEWED SORROW RATHER THAN LAVA

Sagrando did not seem surprised as Lynton flashed her disarming smile his way and said, "Hi there. I think I may have been rude to Mr. Lopez the other night, and I just wanted to stop by and make an apology."

Quinton puffed out his chest and said, "Lekman does not see anyone during the day, but come in my dear. You can apologize to me and I will convey the same to Lekman. He is not a harsh man, nor one to carry a grudge. Please, come on in. We rarely get visitors during the day. It will be delightful to sit and chat with such a lovely young woman."

Lynton was not a woman who generally dressed provocatively. Most days she wore slacks, a blouse that showed little or no cleavage, hair pulled back in a bun and makeup was barely used, if at all. However, on this day, she was prepared for battle.

It has been said that men are visual creatures. Lynton knew that though men were visually acute that they couldn't care less about fashion. This is not to say that a man does not want a woman to look good in the clothes that she wears, it simply means that if the ultimate goal is

LYNTON AND THE VAMPIRE
AT TAGAYTAY MANOR NEAR THE VOLCANO
THAT SPEWED SORROW RATHER THAN LAVA

to command the attention of the male species it will not matter if you are wearing jeans or a formal ball gown. To a man, it is all about how your display your femininity. Lynton was aware that men turn to look at a hint of sexiness a million times faster than a hint of style.

Lynton knew that most men loved a bit of trampy in everything that women wear. The optimum word is hint, so an overly blatant display of being trampy can have the opposite effect. The key she knew was just a hint of naughtiness in her dress. For that reason, she wore a shirt with spaghetti straps and minuscule shorts. Her small, but perky breasts were displayed in a tasteful but alluring fashion. As mentioned, she never wore much makeup, but this day she did darken her eyebrows and use a bit of eyeliner, as she knew looking exotic would make him swoon more and perhaps be willing to open up with some details about he and Lekman's life at Tagaytay Manor, and maybe even share details on where they had been prior to arriving in Tagaytay. Sitting on the red sofa in the drawing room allowed her to demurely display her soft but sinewy thighs and curvaceously muscular calves. She could tell by Quinton's gaze that he was titillated by her looks.

LYNTON AND THE VAMPIRE
AT TAGAYTAY MANOR NEAR THE VOLCANO
THAT SPEWED SORROW RATHER THAN LAVA

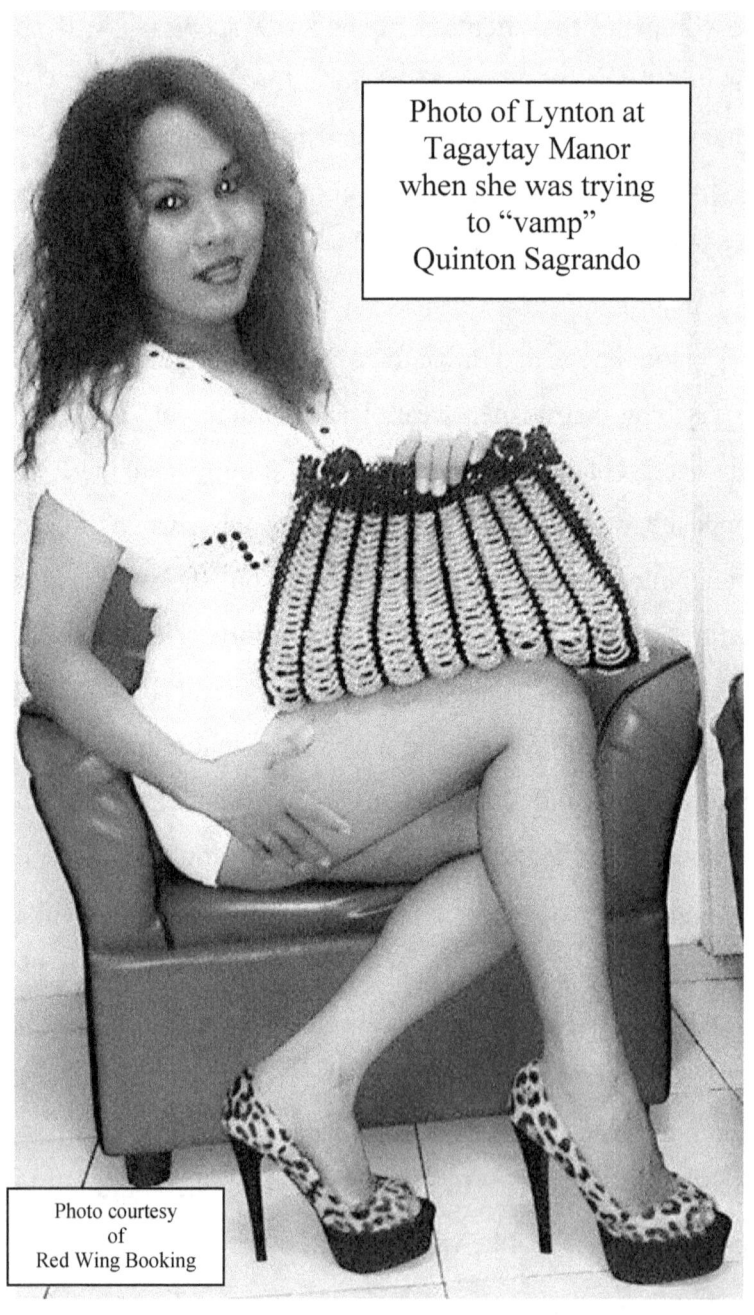

Photo of Lynton at Tagaytay Manor when she was trying to "vamp" Quinton Sagrando

Photo courtesy of Red Wing Booking

LYNTON AND THE VAMPIRE
AT TAGAYTAY MANOR NEAR THE VOLCANO
THAT SPEWED SORROW RATHER THAN LAVA

Very seductively placing her legs so Sagrando could enjoy seeing how silky smooth they were, she smiled provocatively and said, "So, tell me, how long have you and Mr. Lopez been friends?"

Sagrando, not taking his eyes off her legs, said, "We aren't friends really. I am just a loyal servant, have been for hundreds of years."

Lynton, shocked by his admission to being hundreds of years old, although she did not believe it, found his candour interesting. Why was he being so brazen?

"I know you and your friends want to save Lupe from what you think is evil intent, but do not believe all you hear. What I am going to tell you no one will believe, so it no longer matters what you know about Lekman, me and the Perrdonez family. Lekman and I know your reputation, and how you apparently think, even though you are not a believer in demons, that you are a fighter against human demons. Believe me, Lekman, Patrice and I are not human, nor can you defeat us. You go into combat against us, you are going to die, and the death will not be pleasant."

LYNTON AND THE VAMPIRE
AT TAGAYTAY MANOR NEAR THE VOLCANO
THAT SPEWED SORROW RATHER THAN LAVA

Lynton shifted her position, realizing that vamping this man was not possible. He enjoyed looking at her, but he was not about to fall for her charming, alluring attempts to get information. In fact, he was willingly sharing it without her using feminine wiles to elicit it from him. He apparently had concluded, along with Lekman Lopez, that she and her allies could do them no harm. His last comment about their deaths made her think of the horrible way Diana Rodriguez had died, so she said, "I suppose you mean our deaths would be as horrific as Diana's?"

Smiling, Quentin, reached over and took her cell phone which was still in her hand. She did not fight it, just stared wondering his intent when he said, "I want to make sure that none of our conversation is recorded." He then began to pat her down to make certain there were no other recording devices. He lingered an extraordinary as he felt around her breasts, but Lynton simply stared at him without moving or voicing any objections.

Without any tinge of remorse, Quinton said, "She was going to tell to much. She was going to betray Lekman – that could not be allowed."

LYNTON AND THE VAMPIRE
AT TAGAYTAY MANOR NEAR THE VOLCANO
THAT SPEWED SORROW RATHER THAN LAVA

Lynton, not showing any fear, said "You are all demons from the darkest pits of hell. You will pay for your crimes."

A sinister smile crept across Quinton's lips. "We never have paid, and we never will. Go ahead, tell the police that Lekman killed her, mangled her body, drank her blood for nourishment and see if they believe you. Do you know who Lekman really is?

Lynton, with great confidence and determination, replied "I know who he thinks he is. He believes he is Ambrogio."

"My, my, you have done your research. No one has ever defeated Ambrogio – no one! Vlad the Impaler feared him as he feared no other man. Even when the communist empire of the Ceausescu's was falling apart, those who replaced Ceausescu were afraid of him, afraid to even approach the castle that we called home. Why even that buffoon Ronald Reagan knew better than to send assassins against him for fear he might throw his wrath upon the Reagan family. Ambrogio, or as we call him now, Lekman Lopez, is immortal. He has lived for almost 2000 years and will live for another two thousand."

LYNTON AND THE VAMPIRE
AT TAGAYTAY MANOR NEAR THE VOLCANO
THAT SPEWED SORROW RATHER THAN LAVA

Lynton looked around the manor, trying to figure out where Lekman Lopez might be. Was he so deluded that he actually slept in a coffin somewhere in the darkness? Could she get Quinton to reveal his whereabouts? She had no wooden stake, she had no garlic, she did not even have a silver crucifix, only a faux silver one and that was no defence against a man who believed himself a vampire. He would figure out it was a fake. What Lynton needed was a real charm that would make him think twice before attacking her. Yes, he might be deluded, but his delusions could make it possible to keep him at bay.

Quinton got up and said, "I know what you want. You want to know where Ambrogio lies during the day. It is something I will not reveal, because as an Aswang, I am not immortal like he is. I can die eventually, though my life is prolonged through mystical spells that keep Aswangs alive for centuries. I long to be a vampire like he is, as does Patrice, but we are at his service now until he gives us the slow bites over a period of time that does not kill, but eventually turns anyone selected into a child of the night. Others are selected to be special, to be initiated without a bite on their 30th birthday. So chosen is Harold Perrdonez."

LYNTON AND THE VAMPIRE
AT TAGAYTAY MANOR NEAR THE VOLCANO
THAT SPEWED SORROW RATHER THAN LAVA

Lynton was now beginning to understand that all these people were delusional, perhaps made so by the mesmerizing power of Lekman Lopez, or as he was now being called, Ambrogio. Lynton had heard Wayne talk of the modern world as a place where the church, corporations and government had learned the art of massive brainwashing and hypnosis. These two methods of manipulation were everywhere in the modern world, particularly in the USA where corporations had seized the government with the election of Ronald Reagan in 1980. Reagan was a man who, with what was, no doubt, the beginning of Alzheimer's disease in the witch-hunting era of virulent anti-communism in the early 1950's, fallen immeasurably under the spell of the propagandists who practiced the acute brainwashing and mass hypnotism of the American public through fear and intimidation to marry them to an ideal that secured the world for corporate culture. Brainwashing is the more violent and overt method of malevolently influencing people. Hypnosis is a gentler, often stealthy, more seductive method that is practiced on a few rather than the many. Hypnosis is a very deep and subtle alteration or distortion of the brain of a human being so that it responds in certain ways and not in others.

LYNTON AND THE VAMPIRE
AT TAGAYTAY MANOR NEAR THE VOLCANO
THAT SPEWED SORROW RATHER THAN LAVA

Hypnosis is a type of derangement of the brain that is somewhat like a computer virus, and it has two special qualities: Impulses (viruses) are implanted at deep levels and are often completely unseen and usually not understood or even accessible for the average individual. Hypnosis works on levels that are hardly accessible by the average person. This mental virus is designed so that later on in life that a skilled person, such as a hypnotist or other manipulator, can piggyback other viruses or messages onto previous ones. These are called post-hypnotic suggestions.

Those who hypnotize others make small, but important alterations in the mind that those hypnotized are unaware of. Such people include hypnotists, but also professional marketers, politicians, lawyers, and even some doctors and of course, the church and above all, corporations. Even most parents, although perhaps unaware of it, and teachers such as college professors are often adept at sneaking inside the operating system of other people's minds and manipulating it to get people to think a certain way. For example, if your parents are conservative, chances are that you will adopt that same way of thinking once you have gone through the rebellious period and become an adult.

LYNTON AND THE VAMPIRE
AT TAGAYTAY MANOR NEAR THE VOLCANO
THAT SPEWED SORROW RATHER THAN LAVA

It is very important for those who manipulate to get inside a person's head when they are as young as possible, because it is much easier to manipulate an undeveloped mind. For example, children easily believe in fairy tales at a young age, but when they get older they can see through the fantasies they accepted as truth. This is where the skilled manipulator comes into play and uses mass hypnotism as a means to control those who prefer to let others do their thinking for them. Most people are completely unaware that they have turned their minds over to others for complete control.

This all is a diabolical and coordinated effort by the favoured and privileged class to control those of us who simply turn our brains over willingly for manipulation. Advertising is the most perfect example of using hypnotism to convince people that a certain product will miraculously change their lives. The modern corporation hires lackeys to mesmerize the public with what amounts to post-hypnotic suggestions. When the consumer goes into the store, he or she subconsciously picks up a certain brand name product because of what amounts to post-hypnotic suggestion. "Yes," thought Lynton, "Lekman Lopez or Ambrogio would be perfectly at home in the board room of a corporation. This was a man with nefarious intentions, and he had Paul and Patrice Perrdonez as well as Quinton Sagrando hypnotized so thoroughly that they were apparently now beyond any help whatsoever. Their delusions were complete.

At this point, it should be strongly pointed out that despite all the proof piling up on the likelihood of real vampires or real Aswangs being present in the Philippines, none the main principals of this story were willing to accept what, for people like Lupe, were the realities of real vampires and real Aswangs being present in Tagaytay. Sometimes it is the simple mind that can comprehend things better than the more analytical mind. Those given to comprehensive analysis and thought are often bewildered by what some people can believe and how they can blindly follow paths that lead to their own destruction. For example, many people vote on religion. They assume one party loves a certain deity more than another party; consequently; although the party for which they vote loves the deity, the voters own best interests economically might be better served by the party that loves the deity less.

LYNTON AND THE VAMPIRE
AT TAGAYTAY MANOR NEAR THE VOLCANO
THAT SPEWED SORROW RATHER THAN LAVA

Lynton was now convinced she would get very little useful information from Quinton, so she elected to simply throw caution to the wind. She blurted out, "So, Lekman, or now as you say Ambrogio, is going to summon some demons who will make Harold's soul cross over into Ambrogio's body and make him strong and vibrant again."

A look of excitatory anticipation brightened Quinton's face as he replied, "Yes, my master will be good for another 1000 years, and he will offer me and Patrice the bite of immortality as we crossover from our Aswang existence into a more exalted plain. Paul, who is a mortal, unlike us, will have to undergo a more sublime, gradual transformation, but he will, too, one day be exalted as he has agreed to give his son up for the glory of Ambrogio."

Lynton was feeling emboldened now. "So, you are going to let me walk out of here with this knowledge? You have no fear of me going to the authorities, no fear of me finding Ambrogio and driving a stake through his heart? No fear of me encasing him in concrete for eternity? I do know how to kill a vampire you know. I am not ignorant of the rituals, despite thinking they are nothing but myth."

LYNTON AND THE VAMPIRE
AT TAGAYTAY MANOR NEAR THE VOLCANO
THAT SPEWED SORROW RATHER THAN LAVA

Smiling, Quinton moved toward her slowly, and stopped so close to her that she could feel his breath upon her forehead as he looked down on her. "You can be snuffed out right now. I have the power, but I shall not use it, because when I become a vampire, I am going to hunt you down and I shall make you my companion for all eternity. I shall slowly, methodically bite you over a period of time so that you can join me in immortality. I long for the day when we will embrace in vampiric ecstasy, in the rapture of our own blood lust that will nourish us for all eternity."

Lynton, never one prone to profanity, turned and walked toward the door. She looked back over her left shoulder and gazed directly into his eyes and said, "You are one sick asshole."

She looked to her right as she moved toward the door and saw an archway that led down some ancient stone stairs. At the end was a stone door that, no doubt, led to the crypt of one Ambrogio, alias Lekman Lopez, because above the door, inscribed in Latin were just two words: *Deus Fiction*. Attending Catholic Sunday School finally paid off as she remembered her Latin. It translated as *God is Fiction*.

LYNTON AND THE VAMPIRE
AT TAGAYTAY MANOR NEAR THE VOLCANO
THAT SPEWED SORROW RATHER THAN LAVA

Suddenly, a violent, ear shattering scream reverberated all across the giant foyer as Quinton, moving rapidly toward Lynton like a battering ram, head down and face afire with hatred shouted, "Call me an asshole bitch. I will teach you."

Now, if you will remember, Lynton was wearing three inch spiked heels in her attempt to be alluring, which had log ago been cast aside as an exercise in futility. However, as those of you who read *Lynton Walks on Water* know, on Lynton's feet they were more than just a sexy accouterment. These accessories were deadly weapons, which she knew how to use to maximum effect.

One thing most men knew about Lynton was that she was not one with whom you wanted to mess. She was only 5:2 and weighed a mere 50 kilos (about 110 pounds). However, she had been a world class volleyball player, a professional dancer and studied karate in Korea. Put all that together and her legs were lethal weapons, and she knew how to use them with deadly precision. Put some three inch high heels on her and those legs were like a sharp blade that could inflict incredible damage on the unsuspecting.

LYNTON AND THE VAMPIRE
AT TAGAYTAY MANOR NEAR THE VOLCANO
THAT SPEWED SORROW RATHER THAN LAVA

As Quinton raised his head slightly, he was shocked when she, rather than running in fear, turned toward him and greeted his maddening rush with an almost sinister smile of anticipatory glee. She simply pivoted to her left, balancing herself on her muscular left leg as she raised her right leg waist high, pointed the sharp spiked heel at his groin and with a mighty flexing move put her full force behind it in an area where all men are vulnerable. Mr. Battering Ram crumbled to the floor in agonizing pain. As he rolled around gripping his groin, Lynton looked down and said, "Don't bother to show me out, asshole. Oh, excuse me, I am so sorry, I wouldn't want to offend you."

She bent over him for awhile, doing something with his key chain. One large key on the chain was of particular interest to her.

As she walked out into the fading sunlight, she thought to herself, "Hey, even Aswangs are vulnerable to a kick in the groin."

LYNTON AND THE VAMPIRE
AT TAGAYTAY MANOR NEAR THE VOLCANO
THAT SPEWED SORROW RATHER THAN LAVA

CHAPTER 9

TALL TALES FROM BACKWARD MINDS

In my tomb where I await nightly resurrection,

I dwell and search its depths for eternity.

Sorrow bedecks the walls of the odious spot,

When shall I glean aright and stand in grandeur,

The living spectacle of my bitter lot

To meld my handy work and mine eyes delight.

Darkness where I dwell is a magnificent storm.

Ah, I must with caution avoid a brilliant sun;

The mortals wrought such havoc and harm

That of buds on my plot there remains hardly one.

Behold now the fall of ideas I have reached,

And the shovel and rake one must therefore resume,

In collecting the turf, inundated and breached,

Where time dug trenches as deep as my tomb.

And yet these new blossoms, for which I craved,

Will they find in this earth like a shore that is laved

The mystical fuel which vigour imparts?

Oh misery ! Time devours their lives,

And the enemy black, which consumeth my soul

On the blood of their bodies, my heart thrives !

LYNTON AND THE VAMPIRE
AT TAGAYTAY MANOR NEAR THE VOLCANO
THAT SPEWED SORROW RATHER THAN LAVA

Lynton shared all that happened with Channa and Ingrid, and they all laughed with glee at the fate which had befallen Quinton. Channa and Lynton were adamant that there was no such thing as a vampire, but the more religious Ingrid reached into her purse and came out with three solid silver crucifixes she had bought that day in Robinson's Mall. "Ladies," she said with resignation, "I know you are doubters, and that is fine. However, I am arming you with some weapons just in case. Even though they might not be such things as vampires and Aswangs, be assured these deluded people believe that is what they are. For that reason alone, these solid sliver crucifixes might ward them off in dire circumstances."

Channa and Ingrid took them. Then, Ingrid reached in her purse again and came out with three wooden stakes. She handed them to the girls, took one for herself and said, "it might be considered murder if we go on trial, but I had rather take my changes with a judge and jury than be in the arms of that devil Lekman Lopez. He tried to bite me once, but thanks to you two arriving in a timely fashion I was saved. I want all of us to be protected from the evil of this man, so please take these just in case."

LYNTON AND THE VAMPIRE
AT TAGAYTAY MANOR NEAR THE VOLCANO
THAT SPEWED SORROW RATHER THAN LAVA

The girls reached out and took the stakes, and did not hesitate to put them in their waistbands as if they were guns and their waistbands holsters. They felt like those sheriff's in old westerns, only the clock was not ticking toward high noon, but toward midnight. Lynton knew that over that door where the words *Deus Fiction* were engraved insidious evil awaited, and that they would need to summon all their strength to defeat it. Lupe's fate hinged in the balance, as did Harold's and Lupe's daughter Clara who were also at risk. The girls had battled evil before, but never evil as perverse as this.

On the way to Lupe's home to make final preparations, Ingrid sorrowfully praised the bravery of Harold, who was committed to meeting his fate to save Lupe's daughter Clara, and Lupe was now also prepared to do what she must, even sacrifice her own life for that of her beloved daughter. Yet, Lupe was acting strange.

They all gathered at Lupe's house that night at midnight, knowing that the time assigned for them to be at Tagaytay Manor was 2:00 AM, as Harold had been born at 3:48 AM and it was ascribed by the ritual that all must dutifully begin at that time so that the ceremony of renewal for Ambrogio could offer the proper perspective as proscribed by the two demons that were going to be summoned from hell. How these demons would be manufactured troubled Lynton, as she still did not believe the tales of Ambrogio living all these years by drinking the blood of victims regularly.

Little did she know that Wayne had been doing extensive research on strange deaths on a web-site he had reluctantly paid to join. Called vampiremania.com, it listed the strange deaths involving the taking of blood from victims all over the world, and the one area where it occurred most frequently the last eight years was in the Philippines, primarily in the provinces of Quezon, Cavite and Batangas – all within about two to three hours of Tagaytay by car. Wayne, like Lynton, sceptical, but realizing that an open mind was crucial to solving complex dilemmas, plotted on a map all the murders, and postulated that a bat could easily fly all about those provinces within less than an hour. Outrageous he thought, but strange things were occurring that defied explanation and he felt it important to get this information to Lynton as she prepared to go into battle.

LYNTON AND THE VAMPIRE
AT TAGAYTAY MANOR NEAR THE VOLCANO
THAT SPEWED SORROW RATHER THAN LAVA

He tried desperately to call her, but as usual, her phone was turned off. He arrived at the Manila airport at 11:30 PM, hurried through customs and hailed a cab. To his surprise, it was his friend Charlie who had picked him up there on his last visit. It was 12:15 AM and Wayne was frantic to reach Lynton to let her know about all the murders and the danger she was facing, Wayne urged Charlie to get there as quickly as possible. He promised Wayne he could get there in two hours, 3:15AM at the latest. Also, as they sped down the highway, on the radio were reports that Taal Volcano was rumbling to life, but that it apparently was only venting steam at this point.

Wayne had been to Tagaytay often with Lynton, and they both had great affection for the place as it was where they spent the second and third weeks of Wayne's first visit to the Philippines. It was there that their love blossomed, grew and solidified. Wayne thought of something he had once read: *love is the only thing that grows and blossoms without the aid of the seasons.* He was still mystified by why such a beautiful woman wanted him at his age. It was not money, because she made more than he did as a result of a successful career as an entertainer and entrepreneur. Lynton had laughingly told him that she would have to make sure he was not a fortune hunter. Wayne had replied, "I am a fortune hunter, and I have found my fortune in your gorgeous smile, kind manor, sweet demeanour and generous nature."

She had often told him that his words were the grease that oiled the wheels of her affection. His words touched her heart and made her realize that he was a man of deep compassion for the downtrodden who were pushed aside in a world based on greed. Like him, she saw greed as the curse that trapped mankind in an ever downward spiral into selfishness that permanently relegated the many in service to the few. At their last separation, Wayne gently kissed her in the backseat of Channa's car and whispered, "Never have I known the depth of my love until this hour of our separation. Yesterday and today will be a memory I shall cherish, and without you by my side for awhile, I shall dream of tomorrow when you will be in my arms again."

As the cab sped down the toll road, which like everything in the Philippines, was run by corporations, Wayne could only think of what was going on in Tagaytay. Could he get

LYNTON AND THE VAMPIRE
AT TAGAYTAY MANOR NEAR THE VOLCANO
THAT SPEWED SORROW RATHER THAN LAVA

there in time to help fortify Lynton against an evil that she was not completely capable of dealing with. Wayne was a sceptic, but his scepticism did not keep him from understanding that there were forces at work in Tagaytay Manor that Lynton might simply not understand. The knowledge he had of colours that were not discernable to the average person's eye made him think that she might not be able to see the evil because of the "forbidden colours" anomaly. If there were demons, they might not be visible to anyone but vampires and Aswangs, both of which had eyes capable of seeing what others could not see.

Like a bandit preparing to rob a bank, Lynton was preparing, with her gang, to rob Ambrogio of the opportunity to renew his body with the soul of Harold Perrdonez and the life of Lupe. With broad shoulders developed from athletic feats and a body as taunt as an archer's bow pulled back ready to deliver an arrow to the heart of an enemy, she put on her green cloak that waved within the wind and seemed to dance when she walked. Like swaying serpents round entwined magic wands she moved about with a swaying, rhythmic elegance. Like the shifting sands in the deserts remote she floated about with a softness, but mortal suffering would be trampled beneath the biting sand wherein an angel floated in the guise of a woman whose high heels clicked with the symbolic deadliness of she who could be an angel of retribution when called upon. In her long, flowing mien, cold with its silky smooth darkness mingled the mightiness of a sphinx in ancient Egypt. Hers was a countenance of shiny gold, hard steel, polished gems and above all a heavenly light that shined like a million stars to proclaim her majesty.

All those gathered there looked at the clock as it clicked slowly toward 2:00AM and Lynton, staring down at Richie, said "Take care of the children Richie. Yours is the most important task of all. Do not worry, your darling daughter and Lupe will return."

Richie stood, embraced Lupe and thanked Lynton for being such a good friend. He proudly proclaimed, "And no cigarettes despite my nervousness. You Lynton are our saviour. Jesus may be who we pray to in church, but you are out here doing his work every day. Go with my love and the assurance that this family will never forget you and your friends' devotion and kindness."

LYNTON AND THE VAMPIRE
AT TAGAYTAY MANOR NEAR THE VOLCANO
THAT SPEWED SORROW RATHER THAN LAVA

Now, it was obvious that Lynton, Channa and Ingrid would have to break into Tagaytay Manor and clandestinely view the proceedings before coming to rescue of Lupe, her daughter and Harold from the clutches of four people who were hell-bent on carrying out an abominable ceremony that they believed would make them immortal. 3:48 AM was the key, and as the clock slowly ticked toward 3:00 AM, the five stood down the hill from Tagaytay Manor and noticed that there were no lights on upstairs, only the downstairs had one dim light on. Obviously, everyone was in the lower confines of the manor, in the dark tomb behind the door that had carved into stone the words *Deus Fiction*. Perhaps there should have been more words thought Lynton. It would be appropriate to have added *Ibi est et vivit, sed diaboli* (but the devil is alive and well here).

In the foreboding darkness, Lynton surveyed the estate from afar as Harold started up toward the manor in what was the loneliest, most sombre walk of his life, despite the fact that Ingrid had passionately kissed him on the lips and said, "All will be fine, Harold. We three girls have never failed."

LYNTON AND THE VAMPIRE
AT TAGAYTAY MANOR NEAR THE VOLCANO
THAT SPEWED SORROW RATHER THAN LAVA

Lupe watched as Harold was admitted, not by Quinton Sagrando, but by Lekman Lopez, who stood stoically and gazed intrepidly into his eyes. He was quiet obviously hypnotizing Harold, preparing him for the ceremony.

Lupe was strangely calm, and her seeming lack of trepidation was troubling to Lynton because like all mothers when their children are endangered, she should have been displaying outward signs of concern. Lynton was thinking that there are those who seem to believe that children owe their parents for some reason. However, what is owed for bringing someone into the veil of tears called life she thought? It is the parent, thought Lynton, who owes the child that did not asked to be born. Parents are the responsible ones. It is they who must bear the heavy burdens of assistance, not the children. Lynton turned to Lupe, who did not say a word; she took Lupe's hand and looked deep into her eyes. There was coldness there in her suddenly fiery red eyes that troubled Lynton.

In nature's temple, living columns rise, which oftentimes give tongue to words subdued, and man or woman traverses this symbolic mood, which gazes with half familiar eyes.

LYNTON AND THE VAMPIRE
AT TAGAYTAY MANOR NEAR THE VOLCANO
THAT SPEWED SORROW RATHER THAN LAVA

Like lingering echoes, which afar confound themselves in deep and sombre unity as vast as the night, the transplendency and glory of a moment without words can say more than a thousand tongues. This was one of those moments, when Lupe for some reason had changed from demure woman to a woman of immense cold, calculating determination. She pursed her lips together and turned, walking to face an uncertain fate, but still Lynton was troubled by her lack of emotion. Was it because she knew that she had a mighty champion on her side? That she knew that Lynton, along with Ingrid and Channa, was a mighty force against the dark bastions of evil.

Wayne, sitting up front with Charlie, was sharing the details of what was going on with him and why it was so urgent he get to Tagaytay as soon as possible.

Charlie was familiar with stories of Aswangs as he had come up in a province where he said they were prevalent when he was a child. As he was relating tales of horror in the small village he called home then, he let slip a name that brought instant recognition to Wayne, as he had heard it from Lynton in regards to Tagaytay Manor, and the name had also been mentioned by Dr. McCormick. It seems that into Charlie's village a family had moved from Tagaytay at a time when the village was no longer suffering the scourge of Aswang infestation. However, when they came to the village, strange occurrences of a different kind started. The family had moved from Tagaytay when Charlie, who was now 70, was only 12. Yes, it had been over 50 years ago when the Kabian family took up residence there. That name penetrated Wayne's brain and reverberated within it like an echo of recognition, because he knew that tragedy had apparently befallen that family while at Tagaytay Manor.

So now, we share what Charlie related to Wayne, which should explain what had occurred at Tagaytay Manor 58 years before, where evil had dwelled for so long. The darkness of the lonely road to Tagaytay made Wayne, one not given easily to fright, look about at the blackness almost expecting to see the winged children of the night flapping their wings beneath the pale moon. Charlie was measured and precise. "My parents were not affluent like the Kabians, but they had more than most in the village, and we had taken in one of their daughters, whom I had frankly fallen in love with at the tender age of 12. She was

LYNTON AND THE VAMPIRE
AT TAGAYTAY MANOR NEAR THE VOLCANO
THAT SPEWED SORROW RATHER THAN LAVA

14. You see, they were worried about her, and felt the need to escape from Tagaytay because some person who had sinister designs on her was using hypnotism to control her. They came to our village so they might keep her from harm. Remember, this was a time when 14 year old girls, especially in the small villages, were marrying with some degree of regularity. This was an older man of about 40 who had designs on her, and apparently he had so thoroughly mesmerized her that they were afraid she would run off with this visiting Spaniard who cut a rather dashing figure and made all the young girls swoon over him."

Fortunately, Charlie spoke almost perfect English, so Wayne had no problem understanding him as he continued. "The girl's name was Lupe Kabian. Ah, the name still sends waves of passion over me after all these years."

Wayne assumed it was mere coincidence that this girl from over 50 years ago was named the same as the girl who Lynton was now assisting, but as Charlie continued his story, a pattern began to develop and Wayne's scepticism about vampires and Aswangs slowly began to fade. Just as he was concerned about the lack of knowledge Lynton had in regards to certain colours the eye could not perceive, he would begin to realize there were even more profound considerations affecting her safety. So, what follows is the crux of the story as related by Charlie minus a few details that are not relevant.

"So, as I said I was enamoured with her. The Kabian family had left Tagaytay because, as they related to my father, their daughter had simply become so infatuated with this man that their home life had been torn asunder. They had no proof, but they genuinely felt their son's untimely demise from an accident at what is now called Tagaytay Manor was the result of murder by this man named Lekman Lopez. He had been feuding with the girl's 18 year old brother over the relationship, and the boy was found at the bottom of Taal Hill one morning, his skull crushed from a fall, but there was something strange about his body. Almost all his blood had been drained. There were two puncture marks on his neck, and there was very little blood on the ground. A few days later, the girl's other brother who was 21 and had publicly proclaimed Lekman to be a vampire met with an untimely accident also, falling from a horse as he rode home from town. His body, too, had those puncture wounds and had been drained of most of its blood. Again, there was very little blood on the ground. The family simply had enough of living in fear of this man in a community where no one seemed interested in doing anything about it. Consequently, they spirited there daughter and their two remaining children away in the middle of the night and were never heard from there again. Of course, they swore my dad to complete secrecy, but after all these years and the fact that I am sure Lupe is dead, means there should be no harm in my sharing the story with you."

Wayne, enthralled by the story asked, "You assume she is dead. You don't know for certain?"

"No, I do not. All I know is that the Kabians decided to go to America, so fearful they were of this man. However, the girl got terribly sick, meningitis it was, and they left her with a family in Old Bulihan to recuperate. Their ship sank on the way to America and they were all drowned. As far as I know the girl lived with a family in Old Bulihan until she came of age. There were rumours about her never aging and continuing to live there. You know how superstitions develop into urban legends. Nothing to it, of course, but it makes for a good tale late at night when the power goes out during typhoon season."

Wayne was more determined than ever to get to Tagaytay as fast as possible. As he urged Charlie on, even promising to pay any speeding tickets he asked one final question. "So, did this girl have bites also?"

"She did, there were puncture marks on both sides of her neck. There were those in my old village who believed she became an Aswang and, of course, as I said, there were rumours that she never aged beyond 14, but that she eventually married 40 years later, and something unusual happened. Well, unusual for an Aswang that is."

Wayne knew what the answer would probably be, but he asked it anyway. "So, she began to age right? And she had, unlike most Aswangs, children?

Charlie, replied, "Yeah, you heard the rumour too, uh? Well, its all just foolishness anyway. It is nothing but tall tales from backward minds."

LYNTON AND THE VAMPIRE
AT TAGAYTAY MANOR NEAR THE VOLCANO
THAT SPEWED SORROW RATHER THAN LAVA

CHAPTER 10

NOT THE END OF THE TERROR

Oh muse of my heart so fond of palaces old,

Wilt have thou avoid the evil blast,

Amid those tedious nights, with gloom o'ercast,

As a vampire may lay in his coffin so cold ?

Wilt thou thy marbled shoulders then revive

With a nightly ray that which through shutters peep ?

Alas my poor muse what aileth thee now ?

Thine eyes are bedimmed with the visions of night,

And silent and cold I perceive on thy brow

In their turns despair and madness alight.

A succubus green, or a hobgoblin red,

Has it poured o'er thee horror from its urn.

Or the nightmare with masterful bearing hath led

To he whom on blood must be fed.

I wish, as the health-giving fragrance I cull,

That thy breast with strong thoughts could forever be full,

And that rhythmically flowing thy pure fine blood

Could resemble the olden-time metrical-flood,

Where each in his turn reined the father of rhyme

And Ambrogio to hell is cast for all time.

LYNTON AND THE VAMPIRE
AT TAGAYTAY MANOR NEAR THE VOLCANO
THAT SPEWED SORROW RATHER THAN LAVA

The girls watched surprisingly as Lupe walked in without hesitation, almost as if she were going willingly. Why had she been so reluctant and suddenly seemingly embraced the night with Ambrogio? Was she acting her part with skill, or was something amiss?

Channa said, "What goes with that girl? She seems so calm, almost ready to embrace Ambrogio."

"That is of no worry now, Channa" said a perplexed Lynton. "We are going to save a child, save Harold and maybe Lupe, and, in the process, put an end to the skulduggery of Ambrogio - AKA - Lekman Lopez."

Ingrid, with an anticipatory tone, said "And pray tell us dear Lynton, as we have placed all our confidence in you and not even asked of you a detail about how we are to bring this cretin to justice. We await your battle plan."

Smiling, Lynton reached in her pocket and pulled out a key. "When Quinton was writhing in pain from the Lynton Heels from Hell, I simply grabbed my compact, reached down and made an impression in my makeup of something that was obviously the key to the stone door, as it was an old style key as I noticed the old lock on the door. I simply went to the local locksmith and had him make a key from the impression. As for the front door, it is a modern lock and there is no moulding around it, so a credit card slid between the jam and the lock will instantly open it. We go in, unlock the door to Ambrogio's crypt and interrupt the ceremony with these." She held up the wooden stake in one hand and the crucifix in the other. These people are so deranged that they will think we have power over them with these two items. So fearful will they be that we take pictures with our cell phones, threaten to expose them and they will just go quietly into the night they profess to love. We may not be able to pin the murder of Diana Rodriquez on them, but we will have Lupe, her daughter and Harold safe from the clutches of these evil people. Ambrogio will simply disappear from Tagaytay and things will return to normal."

Glancing at her watch, it was now 3:35AM. Lynton said, looking at Channa with a smile, because she was about to use the phrase Channa loved. "Let's go kick some demon butt."

LYNTON AND THE VAMPIRE
AT TAGAYTAY MANOR NEAR THE VOLCANO
THAT SPEWED SORROW RATHER THAN LAVA

Laughing out load, Channa replied "OK, let's do it."

Ingrid chirped in "I live for this kind of thing."

Like marshals or sheriffs in the old Wild West, they strode into the street, looking up at Tagaytay Manor as the volcano whined a lonely rumble of sorrow belching steam into the air. They walked unbowed, unafraid, defiant, proud and bold toward a den of inequity that awaited them. They had no guns, but they had wooden stakes, crucifixes and a commitment to fight injustice as their weapons. These were mighty warriors in the battle of good verses evil. These girls were the battering rams of righteousness in a world ruled by the unrighteous. There cherub like faces belied an iron willed character that simply knew no fear.

Her HSBC credit card worked its magic and the door popped open with ease. They all three looked down at the stone door. Lynton checked her watch – 3:42AM. They moved cautiously to the door and Lynton placed the key in the lock and turned it quietly. She had not been in the crypt, so she did not know what to expect. However, she assumed there would be a vestibule, and true to form, there was.

LYNTON AND THE VAMPIRE
AT TAGAYTAY MANOR NEAR THE VOLCANO
THAT SPEWED SORROW RATHER THAN LAVA

They could hear incantations being read in Latin. Lynton listened carefully, and in shortened form translated for Channa and Ingrid in a barely audible whisper as the three of them hid behind a large stone column completely out of sight. They were going to wait until the right moment, spring upon the miscreants and free those who were hostages to the evil.

Suddenly, the three stared in shock as Lupe fell into the arms of Ambrogio, as if they were passionate lovers. She swooned with delight as he kissed her while Harold, tied to a cross in mock representation of Jesus on Cavalry stared in disbelief while his father and stepmother stood by seemingly rapturously enthralled by the procedures of evil that were methodically unfolding before him. Then the strangest thing of all occurred as Quinton Sagrando opened what appeared to be a giant ancient stone vault behind the altar where Ambrogio was still embracing Lupe, wrapping her in his arms as if they were lovers reunited after years of separation. The vault opened into intense darkness, but one could make out the faint outline of stairs that apparently led deep into the bowels of the earth. The Latin incantations continued as they were summoning demons from the pit of evil at the bottom of the old stone stairs. Did the stairs lead to hell? Was it just demons or the devil himself they were summoning?

Suddenly Ambrogio shouted in Latin, "Arise oh great ones. Step from the chamber that corrals your splendid evil that gives our lives meaning. Show us your fieriness in all its glory so that we may see your seven heads of splendorous malevolent loathsomeness. We worship at your altar great one. We bow in supplication to your superiority of evil which will rule with a mighty sword of retribution over the heads of all who do not heed your magnificence. Come forth, come forth and embrace us, give us immortality so that we may serve you for eternity in glorious submission to your will."

Then, Lynton, reviled in shock when she heard two demons' names pour forth from Ambrogio's mouth like a cesspool of evil. They were summoning two of the vilest demons imaginable. OK, it might be all make-believe, all nothing but the manifestations of deranged minds, but they certainly knew their demons, and the two they called were the most horrendous imaginable – Lamashtu and Belphego.

LYNTON AND THE VAMPIRE
AT TAGAYTAY MANOR NEAR THE VOLCANO
THAT SPEWED SORROW RATHER THAN LAVA

All those gathered there fell to their knees and were worshipping non-existent entities. The three girls stood mystified at how all these lunatics could be bowing before what amounted to thin air. All of them were enthralled and bowing in supplication, even Harold, who was securely fastened to the cross seemed to be eyeing intently that which was not there. Channa shrugged her shoulders and said, "These people have gone off the deep end. They are all candidates for the funny farm."

This particular day, the sun was scheduled to come up at 5:45AM, and, without realizing it, the girls had been so mesmerized and thoroughly captivated by what was occurring that they had lost all track of time. Lynton looked down at her watch and it was 5:30 – way past time for them to break up the gathering and stop the nonsense and free Lupe's daughter, who, sitting over in a far corner, seemed as hypnotically focused on the proceedings as were the others, and what was even stranger was that the .little girl was not even tied up. Had they somehow convinced her that she was also an Aswang or vampire?

Now, while all this was going on, the reader needs to reflect on what was said about certain colour hues never being seen by the human eye. Something was about to occur that would lead to a startling discovery and permanently alter Lynton's perception of reality.

LYNTON AND THE VAMPIRE
AT TAGAYTAY MANOR NEAR THE VOLCANO
THAT SPEWED SORROW RATHER THAN LAVA

Wayne had arrived at the manor after trying to locate Lynton at several other places. After bidding Charlie goodbye, he walked through the open door, heard the loud noises emanating from the basement and proceeded down the stairs where he saw the three girls peering from behind the column. He moved over to them and a surprised Lynton whispered. "Baby, I am glad to see you, but surprised. These crazy people think that they are actually talking to two demons."

Wayne looked at the proceedings and said, "And what demon or demons have they summoned? Let me guess – Lamashtu and Belphegor."

Surprised, the three girls nodded affirmatively. Wayne whispered "Lamashtu is a heinous, terrifying, demoness. She is said to menace women in particular by kidnapping infants while they're breastfeeding so she can suck their blood, and chew on their bones. She, when unable to find infants for blood sucking, sucks the blood of men and spreads diseases and illnesses. And, unlike most demons, she does not answer to anyone; not even the devil, or any hierarchal evil entity. So evil is Lamashtu that other demons often avoid her She is usually described as a mythological hybrid, with the head of a lioness, the teeth

LYNTON AND THE VAMPIRE
AT TAGAYTAY MANOR NEAR THE VOLCANO
THAT SPEWED SORROW RATHER THAN LAVA

and ears of a donkey, the feet of a bird, complete with sharp talons, as well as a hairy body, and long, sharp fingers and fingernails. Belphegor is associated with orgies, and other types of lewdness. The Israelites worshiped him, in the form of a phallic idol. He seduces with money and overall wealth. He requires human sacrifice. He is a hideous, bearded demon with horns and claws. However, the real crux of what I am saying is that they are here now. These people are worshipping them, and because they are Aswangs and vampires, they can see them – you and I cannot, because there are two hues of colours the human eye cannot see. Lamashtu is blue-yellow and Belphegor is reddish green. You think the demons are not here, but they are, I assure you. They are!"

Frantic, Lynton said, "What do we do?"

Wayne said, "You, no doubt have crucifixes. Use them to ward off the evil temporarily. The demons are affected by them too. I will quickly untie Harold, run out with Lupe and her daughter. None of the others, including Ambrogio, will be able to follow as long as a crucifix is between them and the doorway. Are you ready?"

LYNTON AND THE VAMPIRE
AT TAGAYTAY MANOR NEAR THE VOLCANO
THAT SPEWED SORROW RATHER THAN LAVA

Ingrid shouted "hell yes" so loud that those present heard then and turned in their direction. Wayne rushed for Harold, quickly untied him, while in the confusion, Lupe grabbed her daughter and ran up the stairs. As Harold was climbing the stairs, the girls, crucifixes in hand held them out in front of them as they stood between Paul, Patrice, Quinton and Ambrogio. They, of course, could not see the demons but could actually hear their hissing noises, now. Paul came at Lynton with the ritual stone knife which was lying on the altar. She raised her deadly right high heel up level with her right shoulder as she stood unwavering on her left leg and buried her heel in his heart, pulling it out instantly and pivoting to her left where she buried it this time in Patrice's stomach. Meanwhile, Quinton Sagrando was scurrying down the vault stairs to escape the wrath, as apparently, although unseen, also were the two demons. Wayne quickly closed and locked the vault door assured that they were where they belonged now – in hell.

As Harold and Lupe ran frantically up the stairs, Ambrogio's mesmerizing eyes caught Harold's attention when he turned around to look back. He wobbled and tumbled head first down the stairs. From the snapping noise

LYNTON AND THE VAMPIRE
AT TAGAYTAY MANOR NEAR THE VOLCANO
THAT SPEWED SORROW RATHER THAN LAVA

it was obvious he had broken his neck. As Harold lay dead at the the foot of the stairs, Lupe continued her mad dash with her daughter out of Tagaytay Manor. She had to get home as quickly as possible to do something.

Through all this, Ambrogio stood in stoic resolution as his world of evil was tumbling all about him. He bowed his head, wrapped his cloak around himself and a bat materialized flapping its wings violently it flew up the stairs. Wayne turned to the three girls and said, "I know you have stakes. Drive them through the hearts of Paula and Patrice just in case."

Wayne shouted as he ascended the stairs, "With Ambrogio loose, Lupe and her family are in danger. I must get to her house.

The ramming of the stakes through the hearts was done so quickly that the girls almost instantly were behind Wayne, and as they got to the top of the stairs they were greeted by the morning sun and Ambrogio pleading with the girls who were holding crucifixes in front of themselves in extended arms, to let him by so that he could return to the basement and darkness. He was so weak that his voice was hardly audible.

A scent of burning rubber penetrated the nostrils of those there, as Ambrogio was now back in human form and slowly wilting away, seemingly dissipating before their eyes. Finally, he was gone and nothing but dust lay on the floor.

On earth Ambrogio, a Vampire is sent.
His corpse from his tomb was for rent
To ghastly haunt from place to place
and suck the blood of the human race.
There from daughter, husband and wife
At midnight did he drain the stream of life.
Upon a human banquet he did perforce,
Feeding on that which was now a living corpse.
The victims did eventually expire,
As blood filled the mouth of the sire.
Cursed was he while cursing them.
His flowers withered on the stem.
Now he lies as dust from the sun.
His deadly reign is done.

LYNTON AND THE VAMPIRE
AT TAGAYTAY MANOR NEAR THE VOLCANO
THAT SPEWED SORROW RATHER THAN LAVA

Ingrid returned to the bottom of the stairs, resting Harold's head in her hands as Channa and Ingrid tried to console her. They gradually weaned her from him, leading her up the stairs where they stood staring down at what was left of Ambrogio.

Evil comes through stone walls, darkens the light of day, and rarely makes its exit before severe damage is done. Ambrogio had proved the destructive power of evil, but it had also cost him his immortality.

A block of stone could not have been more still than the stillness which permeated about Channa, Ingrid, Lynton and Wayne as they all breathed a sigh of collective relief that the ordeal was over and the evil finally lay dormant for ever as the one sure fire way of getting read of a vampire by exposing it to light had destroyed Ambrogio for all time.

There was not the slightest stir of respiration. As the four of them stared at the dust, it appeared to have changed its place, and was now nearer the door; then, close to it. The door was open, and the dust passed through the archway as a gust of wind spread the ashes all about.

LYNTON AND THE VAMPIRE
AT TAGAYTAY MANOR NEAR THE VOLCANO
THAT SPEWED SORROW RATHER THAN LAVA

Terror is usually a transitory occurrence, and though these four were brave, they were not immune to fright. What they had seen was probably the most frightening experience of their lives. Three people lay dead downstairs, another person had descended into the fiery pit with the demons, and Ambrogio was now nothing but dust and a woman and her child had fled to safety. Yet, what these four had seen was not the end of the story, not the end of the terror.

LYNTON AND THE VAMPIRE
AT TAGAYTAY MANOR NEAR THE VOLCANO
THAT SPEWED SORROW RATHER THAN LAVA

EPILOGUE
TAAL RUMBLED

The sun peeps over the horizon enveloped in crape.

Sun of daytime life wrap thyself up in shade;

At will, smoke or slumber, be silent, be staid,

And dive deep down in dispassion's dark pit.

Aswangs cherish thee thus! But if 'tis thy mood,

Like a star that from out its penumbra appears,

To float in the regions where madness careers,

Fair dagger burst forth from where thy stood.

Light up thine eyes at the fire of renown!

Or kindle desire by the looks of some clown!

Thine flight is joy, whether dull or aflame!

Just be what thou wilt, black night, dawn divine,

There is not a nerve in my trembling frame

But cries, "take flight as the evil is thine!"

At first, there was no need to rush to Lupe's home they all thought, but as Wayne related the story of the Aswang that had been adopted and lived for so many years. As Charlie had said, for years she appeared to never age beyond 14, but that she eventually married 40 years later to

LYNTON AND THE VAMPIRE
AT TAGAYTAY MANOR NEAR THE VOLCANO
THAT SPEWED SORROW RATHER THAN LAVA

a man in Tagaytay and something unusual happened for an Aswang, as unlike most Aswangs, she had children – six to be exact.

They all looked at one another, reflecting on what might be happening down the road from Tagaytay Manor. Thus, their strides became more and more pronounced as the terror returned with their realization that things were far from being as they seemed.

Wayne took Lynton's hand as the mighty four moved unafraid ever forward toward the terror that waited. Wayne looked at Lynton with eyes ablaze with affection, for in times of trouble, we all seek out those whom we love for solace in our period of turmoil. She stood by his side now, her eyes shining a beacon of hope, as if she was inspired by an angel. Lynton was Wayne's diamond mine and poured out the treasure to Wayne's heart. His transgressions were always forgiven by Lynton for within those eyes that were mystic beams burning radiant and full of love like the sun beating a gracious benevolence. From dark oblivion she had resurrected his soul, and together a spirit of love they proclaimed. Nothing could ever kill their love's flame.

LYNTON AND THE VAMPIRE
AT TAGAYTAY MANOR NEAR THE VOLCANO
THAT SPEWED SORROW RATHER THAN LAVA

Majestically beautiful, the morning of serenity broke as if by some angelic decree heaven's blue hope opened up to embrace these four. Worried mortals dreamed and aspired, and these four were pure of heart, but knew the chasm of despair. Yet, they were intrinsically aware that being pure did not hide them from the blackness of misery and sorrow.

Suddenly, a cloud edged over the sun and darkness seemed to surround them as they moved toward Lupe's open door. Sounds were non-existent and even their strides of assurance evaporated like a melancholy waltz of lost hope. The sun that peered through the window cast an eerie glow upon that which was on the floor. Lying there was Richie, his neck ripped open on both sides as if animals had bitten at it in a feeding frenzy. The sun began to take on a crimson blood-like brine colour as the slow moving cloud almost completely covered it.

All four of them stared out the open window at the sun that was now so crimson that it reminded one of blood dripping endlessly from a wound, and these four were wounded deep within, especially the three girls who had devoted themselves to Lupe who had deceived them.

LYNTON AND THE VAMPIRE
AT TAGAYTAY MANOR NEAR THE VOLCANO
THAT SPEWED SORROW RATHER THAN LAVA

Yes, Lupe was an Aswang, as she had been the girl adopted who stayed forever 14 until she finally wound up in the care of Anna, who probably took her from her mother as her mother had taken her from hers. Thus, Lupe had been doomed from the very beginning, and now she had killed he whom she had married as even love could not keep her from satisfying her blood lust.

The mighty Taal Volcano began to rumble mercilessly, but it did not spew lava, rather it spewed sorrow as the four looked up at the cloud-covered sun and saw one giant bat winging its way across the horizon followed by six smaller bats.

THE END

If you liked this Lynton adventure, don't miss these exciting *LYNTON* books by J. Wayne Frye

LYNTON CURLS HER HAIR

**LYNTON BUYS A NEW CELL-PHONE
AND HEARS THE VOICE OF DOOM**

**LYNTON WALKS ON WATER WHILE
INGRID AND CHANNA DO
AN IRISH JIG**

Available at your local bookstore or at
Amazon.com

**LYNTON AND THE VAMPIRE
AT TAGAYTAY MANOR NEAR THE VOLCANO
THAT SPEWED SORROW RATHER THAN LAVA**

**Don't miss J. Wayne Frye's book that has been called
the modern day *TO KILL A MOCKINGBIRD*
from**
Fireside Books.

HOCKEY MANIA AND THE MYSTERY OF NANCY RUNNING ELK

This is a book about what many people consider the greatest of all sports. Yet, it is more than a story about hockey and its power to bring out the very best in people. Like *TO KILL A MOCKINGBIRD*, this is a story of how a few people in a small town stand up to prejudice and racial inequality. Through an incredible hockey team, issues of class, courage, inequality, compassion and gender roles are explored with an undercurrent plea for tolerance and justice It is a coming of age saga about Monte and Ted, two young hockey players on a town team that has a new coach who has vowed to turn what is termed an un-coachable pack of rogues into a cohesive team of winners. These boys become enamoured with a young Cree maiden who has a dark secret that has kept her on the periphery of respectability for many years. Is she really the dark force of evil that so many portray her to be? One of the two young men will find out much more than expected when going in search of the truth.

Don't miss the classic murder mystery
by J. Wayne Frye

WHITE METEORS
AND THE GHOST
OF
SUE ANN McGEE

A mystery that deals with a murder in a small North Carolina town., like Harper Lee's *TO KILL A MOCKINGBIRD*, this is a book that goes beneath the surface of life in a small southern town to expose the inherent evil of prejudice and to show how the courage of a few can rally people to take a stand against injustice. In 1963, Aaron Adams and Casey Felton embark on a quest to expose vile, insidious evil that would shock the citizens of Asheboro, North Carolina. In the process, a budding romance develops and these two will learn that one of those buried in the town's cemetery refuses to rest quietly in the grave until justice is served. A ghostly apparition brings death and destruction, but Casey and Aaron know that the destruction is only a precursor of a more deadly rampage that will sweep Asheboro into turmoil as it comes to grips with murder most foul.

From

Fireside Books

Available at your local bookstore or on-line

from

amazon.com

LYNTON AND THE VAMPIRE
AT TAGAYTAY MANOR NEAR THE VOLCANO
THAT SPEWED SORROW RATHER THAN LAVA

VOCABULARY (From Merriam-Webster Canadian Dictionary)

PROLOGUE:
euphoric – extremely happy
grandeur – state of being great or magnificent
insipient – becoming apaprent
CHAPTER 1:
sublime – subtle, beneath the surface,
modulate – to change or adjust
manifestations – something appears, often ghost
mortified – to destroy the functioning of, scared beyond belief
envious – jealous of
malicious – with intent to harm
innate – the essential nature of something, usually present from birth
amulet – a small object worn for protection
talisman – an object that is charm for good luck
Usog – Filipino "evil eye" hex
Balius – Same as above
Masamangmata – Tagalog for "stranger with an evil eye"
Mal de Ojo – Spanish for "the evil eye"
CHAPTER 2:
charlatans – one who uses pretexts to take advantage of people
hiatus – a break from
stead – to be in good standing
mosaic – something made of different things that form a pattern
sustenance – means of support, often referring to food needed
cul de sac – street or passage closed at one end
imbued – permeate or inlfluence
barangay – administrative term for a village in Philippines
permeated – to pass or spread through
homogeneous – of a similar kind or nature
spontaneity – undetermined action or movement
malcontent – one who bears a grudge or grievance
portended – a warning
Jeepney – Filipino vehicle that carries passengers (like a bus)
trepidation – anxious about or fearful of something happening
piqued – an arousal of interest, often causing anger
germane – pertaining to
suffice – as much as needed
endemic – characteristic or prevalent to a certain thing or field
sinewy – strong, tough
wrought – deeply stirred

LYNTON AND THE VAMPIRE
AT TAGAYTAY MANOR NEAR THE VOLCANO
THAT SPEWED SORROW RATHER THAN LAVA

sojourn – a stay, usually temporary, somewhere
unfettered – free and unrestained
vassal – one in a subservient or servant-like position who does a deed
riff-raff – disreputable person, sometimes used to describe "common"
CHAPTER 3
inane – lacking significance
intonated – to utter or suggest
portend – to give an omen or anticipatory sign
tribulation – unhappiness, pain or suffering
consternation – amazement or dismay that confuses
defile – to make unclean, impure or to show no respect for something
monoliths – very large or powerful organization
fodder – material used to feed or can refer to useless material
euphoria – extreme happiness
soiree – a party or reception usually held in the evening
Kumusta – what's up in Filipino
palpitating – to beat quickly or strangly
rapacious – always wanting more
libido – sexual drive
ductile – easily led or influenced, easy to fashion into
fibrously – containing, resembling or consisting of fibers
derriere – the buttock (French term)
painstakingly – with great care
penchant – strong inclination for or ability at soemthing
crème de la crème – the very best
CHAPTER 4:
benignant – serenely mild and kind
Savoir-faire – cool, knowing what to do in any situation, confident
suave –relaxed, confident with great self assurance
epigrammatic – compact, crisp observation
persona – the way you behave
intonated – implied
stupefying – groggy, insensible
discombobulated – upset, confused
exactitude – the quality of being exact
intermittently – coming or going at intervals
effaced – to eliminate or wear away
precipitously – happening quickly or suddenly
disconsolate – cheerless, unhappy
realm – a field or domain of activity (a kingdom)
CHAPTER 5:

LYNTON AND THE VAMPIRE
AT TAGAYTAY MANOR NEAR THE VOLCANO
THAT SPEWED SORROW RATHER THAN LAVA

chagrin – distressed, embarrassed, humiliated
henchmen – a faithful follower or supporter
stratagem – a plan or scheme, usually to deceive
husband – to use cautiously, to conserve your energy, to call upon
anonymity – not being known
clandestinely – done without being known or seen
cerebral – using your head
claptrap – foolish or stupid use of words
caveats – a qualification or clarification
lament – regret
obeisance – a gesture showi9gn respect
CHAPTER 6:
cow-tow – going overboard in showing respect
pestilential – annoying
pyre – a pile or heap of combustible material or body
consecrated – respectful, usually religious respect use of
anachronism – belonging to a prior time, not usual for today
penchant – habitual liking of something or some way of doing
pervasive – spreading wildly
skewed – twist or turned
cursory – hasty, not detailed
ferreting – search or discover
veneration – to hold in high esteem
exemplary – serving as a desirable model
bombastic – high sounding, iflated but of little meaning
postulated – suggest or assume a fact
discourse – thoughts, ideas usually through a long talk
pompous – arrogant, self-importance
aggrandizement – high praise
oration – an oral presentation on a worthy theme
potentate – a monarch or ruler with great power
decorum – behaviour that is proper and in good taste
per se – Lain phrase meaning "in itself"
disconcerted – to disturb the composure of
tenuous – weak or slight
CHAPTER 7:
dissipate – disperse or scatter
machinations – scheming or crafty action to accomplish evil ends
incredulity – unable or unwilling to believe something
mayhem – a situation involving great violence or upheaval
languor – stillness in air, tiredness of someone

LYNTON AND THE VAMPIRE
AT TAGAYTAY MANOR NEAR THE VOLCANO
THAT SPEWED SORROW RATHER THAN LAVA

perpetrated – carry our or commit
perpetrators – those who carry out an act
genuflexions – bendign the knee or touching ground in reverence
CHAPTER 8:
enwreathe – surround or encircle sometimes with a wreathe
frivolity – light-hearted happiness
foyer – open area near an entrance
candour – frank, open, honest
wiles – devious or cunning in manipulating people
faux – imitation, false
lackeys – a servant or someone who behaves in a servile manner
nefarious – wicked or criminal actions
accouterment – additional items or equipment for an activity
CHAPTER 9:
postulated – assume or suggest something is a fact
demeanour – outward look or bearing
countenance – a person's facial expression
abominable – very bad or unpleasant
transplendancy – splendid tot eh highest degree
scourge – great trouble or suffering
bastions – a strong defence or standing up for principles
asunder – into pieces
CHAPTER 10:
Succubus – a female demon or supernatural entity
hobgoblin – a troublesome creature
skulduggery – underhanded or unscrupulous behaviour
cretin – a stupid person
inequity – lack of fairness or justice
cherub – type of angel usually shown as a young child
vestibule – a lobby or outer room before the main room
miscreants – a person who behaves badly or breaks the law
rapturously – full of feeling manifesting great joy or delight
malevolent – wishing to do evil
emanating – originate from
hierarchical - arranged in order of rank
phallic – resembling a phallus (penis)
EPILOGUE:
Penumbra – distinct parts of a shadow
chasm – deep difference in views as in a deep fissure in the earth
intrinsically – naturally

www.ingramcontent.com/pod-product-compliance
Lightning Source LLC
Chambersburg PA
CBHW060807120626
46557CB00001B/113